NO TIME TO LOSE

"I'm going to open the screen door real fast," Frank whispered to Chet. "You think you can kick the front door open?"

"No sweat," Chet answered.

Frank peered back in through the window and saw Joe peek around the corner of the inner room. That was what he had been waiting for. He pulled the screen door, and it creaked loudly.

"Now!" he barked to Chet.

Chet planted his foot next to the door knob, then kicked hard. The door groaned and snapped open.

Frank dashed in and confronted the figure sitting in the chair.

"Frank!" Joe shouted. "It's Callie."

Frank would have been relieved to find his girlfriend, but the digital timer on the bomb that was ticking at her feet showed that in thirty seconds they would all be dead.

Books in THE HARDY BOYS CASEFILES® Series

Available from ARCHWAY Paperbacks

THE HARDY BOYS CASEFILES NO. 39

FLESH AND BLOOD

FRANKLIN W. DIXON

AN ARCHWAY PAPERBACK
Published by POCKET BOOKS

New York   London   Toronto   Sydney   Tokyo   Singapore

AN ARCHWAY PAPERBACK *Original*

An Archway Paperback published by
POCKET BOOKS, a division of Simon & Schuster Inc.
1230 Avenue of the Americas, New York, NY 10020

ISBN: 0-671-73913-5

First Archway Paperback printing May 1990

10 9 8 7 6 5 4 3 2

THE HARDY BOYS, AN ARCHWAY PAPERBACK
and colophon are registered trademarks of Simon & Schuster Inc.

THE HARDY BOYS CASEFILES is a trademark
of Simon & Schuster Inc.

Printed in the U.S.A.

IL 7+

FLESH AND BLOOD

Chapter

1

"THIS IS WORSE than a nightmare!"

Frank Hardy brushed back his wet brown hair and scanned the area. The scene looked more like a set for a war movie than downtown Bayport. Several buildings had been leveled, cars had been thrown about like toys, and traffic signs were twisted into pretzel shapes.

What stunned Frank even more was the fact that the destruction had been caused by a tornado.

Tornado? Frank thought with a shake of his head. He had seen pictures of tornadoes hitting places like Oklahoma but not in New York and especially not in a coastal city like Bayport. A hurricane would have been more natural.

A shout snapped Frank from his thoughts.

"Over here!" Joe Hardy was standing next to Chet Morton, waving for Frank to join them.

1

Frank rushed to his younger brother. If Joe could see himself in a mirror, Frank thought, he wouldn't believe it. Always particular about his appearance, Joe looked like a wet mop now. His water-drenched clothes hung on him like soggy rags, and his blond hair was matted flat on his scalp.

"I think I heard someone under this roof," Chet, the Hardys' best friend, explained as Frank joined them.

Frank scanned the red-shingled, fifteen-foot section of roof lying on the pavement. The roof had once covered the Bayport Pawn Shop. The tornado had ripped the roof off and thrown it to the ground.

"If anyone is trapped under there," Frank said, "he can't be alive."

The roof was made of thick plywood covered over with several layers of shingles. Bricks from the building had fallen onto the roof, adding to its crushing weight. Frank wasn't looking forward to seeing what was under the roof.

Frank knelt down and slid his hands under the plywood. "Lift on three," he told Joe and Chet.

Joe and Chet ran to the corners to distribute the weight of the roof evenly.

Frank counted three, and they lifted, grunting and straining. Slowly the roof cleared the ground with a creak and a groan. A bloody hand shot out from the side.

"Chet and I can hold it," Joe said quickly, his

voice straining from the weight. "You pull him out—but hurry."

Frank squatted and grabbed the hand.

"Help me," a man's desperate voice moaned. *"Please."*

Frank knew that moving the man might cause him further injury, but he also knew that Joe and Chet couldn't hold the roof for more than a few seconds longer. Their faces were already deep red from straining. He made a quick decision.

Frank pulled the man free just before the roof fell with a groaning crash.

"Good timing," Joe said, huffing. His face was still red, his breath coming in gasps. "Is he okay?"

Frank felt the man's pulse. "It's weak."

Frank turned toward Chet. "Chet. Call an ambulance."

Chet didn't answer. He was holding his left hand, grimacing as he looked at his index finger.

"What's wrong?" Joe asked.

"I smashed my finger when we dropped the roof," Chet said with a moan. "It feels like it's going to throb off." He started for the van. "I'll call the ambulance."

"Use the CB," Frank called after Chet. "The tornado knocked out the microwave tower, and the cellular phone is dead."

"Okay!" Chet shouted back, still cradling his left hand.

3

"Great job, guys. This ought to make the lead on tonight's news." Callie Shaw walked briskly up to Frank and Joe, her camcorder held firmly against her face, the red On light flashing. "I got the whole rescue on tape."

"Ever since you got that 'newshawk' job, you think you're a national newscaster," Joe quipped. Callie had recently been hired as a video newshawk —an amateur news reporter—for WBAY and was looking for her first story.

"This is the last time I make you a hero, Joe Hardy." Callie turned the camcorder directly on Joe and moved the camera up and down, capturing Joe's wet-cat appearance on videotape. "Wait until the girls get an exclusive look at you, Bayport's most eligible bachelor."

"Hey!" Joe yelled and made a move toward Callie, who dodged Joe's grasp.

Chet rejoined the group. "The ambulance is on its way. I thought he could use this." Chet handed Frank an army blanket from the van.

Frank spread the blanket over the man and reached for his pulse again. He glanced up at Joe and Callie. Callie's mocking smile and Joe's glare told Frank that things were slowly getting back to normal. Not even the presence of a freak early summer tornado could keep Joe and Callie from getting on each other's nerves.

Frank, Joe, Chet, and Callie had been on their way out of Bayport toward the beach when they heard the tornado warning over the radio. At first, none of them believed it. Then, as they were heading back toward town, they watched in horror as the twister hit. Its angry twisting black funnel cloud snaked out of the sky, with furious winds striking a deadly swath one hundred yards wide and four miles long.

They had returned to Bayport and started helping the police and fire departments to search for people trapped in buildings. Callie picked up a camcorder at the TV studio and rejoined the boys in her car.

"Frank! Joe!" a girl yelled from behind them.

The group turned. Don West and Liz Webling trotted up. Liz was an old friend of the Hardys and had helped them on one of their cases, *See No Evil*. Joe had once thought of dating Liz. She was smart, athletic, and enjoyed sporting events, but what Joe liked best about Liz was her shiny short blond hair, large hazel eyes, and terrific figure.

The only thing stopping Joe was Don West. Don had lived in Bayport for three years and had been going steady with Liz for almost two. At six feet, Don was as tall as Joe, just as muscular, and every bit as good-looking. Callie often teased Joe that Don, with his steel gray eyes and long brown hair, was fast replacing Joe as Bayport's heartthrob.

Liz and Don had also been helping in the search for victims. They were working one block over from the Hardys.

"Did you reach your father?" Liz asked Joe.

"Not yet," Joe replied. "The phone lines are down."

"Use your CB," Don suggested. "You could reach a ham operator, and then he could call your dad."

"Good idea," Frank said. "Thanks, Don." He ran to the van.

"I was about to suggest that," Joe said.

"Sure you were," Callie teased.

Joe glared at Callie.

Frank and Joe's father, Fenton Hardy, was in Philadelphia testifying at a trial. The Hardys' mother, Laura Hardy, and their aunt Gertrude had gone with him.

"Find anything?" Callie asked Liz.

"No, thank goodness," Liz replied, looking at the man under the blanket. "Is he okay?"

"We think he will be," Joe replied. "We dragged him out from under that roof."

"Looks heavy," Liz said.

"Not really," Joe said with a shrug.

"Does my finger look blue to you guys?" Chet asked, holding up his swollen index finger.

"No," Joe said with a smirk. "It looks just as happy as the other nine."

Chet stared blankly at Joe for a second, then his face screwed into a frown. "Ha, ha," he said slowly. "You're a regular comedian."

"Whoever heard of a tornado hitting Bayport?"

Callie asked. It was a question that had been on all of their minds, but one for which nobody had an answer.

"Hey, look over there," Liz said, pointing down the street.

They all turned.

"Looks like Mangieri's using his five-finger discount credit card again," Joe said.

Martin Mangieri was just climbing out through the smashed front window of an expensive appliance store with a portable television in his arms.

Joe easily recognized the short, overweight teenager by his long hair, which had the texture and color of dirty yellow wall insulation and was pulled back into a ponytail. Even on a perfect summer day he was wearing his scuffed black leather jacket with the gory hand-drawn skull and crossbones on the back.

Mangieri had been a troublemaker at Bayport High and had been kicked out of school earlier in the year for breaking into the soft drink and candy machines in the student lounge.

"Let's cancel his credit card," Don suggested.

Joe was surprised at Don's suggestion. He had never known the quiet senior to be adventuresome.

"You're on," Joe replied with a wink. "Last one to the creep is a rotten egg." With that, Joe sprinted toward Mangieri.

"Hey!" Don shouted and then started after Joe. A moment later he was next to the younger Hardy.

Joe was surprised at Don's speed and wondered why Don hadn't played football or gone out for track.

They were ten yards from Mangieri when the small-time hood spun around. His face turned a ghostly shade of white, his jaw dropped, and his eyes widened into two large circles of fear. He threw the television at Joe and Don and then darted down the street.

In unison, Joe and Don hurdled the television as it smashed onto the concrete sidewalk.

Although short and fat, Mangieri was fast. He's probably had plenty of practice running from police, Joe thought.

Joe pumped his arms faster and began to gain on Mangieri. He glanced to the side and was pleased to see that Don was lagging behind.

Joe was an arm's length away when Mangieri suddenly stopped, twisted around, and planted a solid right into Joe's stomach. Joe gasped as the air was knocked out of him and he crashed to the ground.

Mangieri ran a half block farther and disappeared into an alley.

"I'll get him," Don announced, sprinting past Joe.

Joe jumped up and instantly wished he hadn't as his stomach muscles contracted from the pain of Mangieri's blow. He was embarrassed that a runt like Mangieri had outmaneuvered him. His embarrassment kindling his anger, he dashed up the street and into the alley down which Mangieri and Don had disappeared.

The alley was a dead end—and it was empty.

Joe moved slowly through the brick corridor, every nerve in his body tense. He listened for any movement.

The alley served as a back exit for several businesses and was lined with trash dumpsters. It ended at the back wall of another building.

Joe was halfway down the alley when he was grabbed and jerked to the side. Joe hit the wall, the breath nearly knocked out of him again. He clenched his fist.

"Not so fast, Joe," Don whispered.

"What?"

"Shhh." Don raised a finger to his lips.

"Where's Mangieri?" Joe angrily whispered.

Don nodded toward a dumpster directly across from them.

Joe peered at the dumpster. A bit of black leather jacket hung out between the dumpster and its lid.

"You want to do the honors, or shall I?" Don asked.

Joe rubbed his sore stomach. "I will," he growled.

Joe walked over to the dumpster and threw up the lid.

Mangieri popped up like a jack-in-the-box, swinging a piece of wood straight at Joe's head. Joe saw the blurred board in time and ducked. The force of Mangieri's swing and miss unbalanced the overweight thief, and he spun around and fell backward head over heels out of the dumpster.

Mangieri scrambled to his feet. Joe grabbed for the worm, but Mangieri wiggled free and planted a solid left to Joe's already sore gut.

Joe groaned and clamped his hands on Mangieri's black leather jacket. Twice Mangieri had outmoved him. Joe yanked Mangieri up until the punk was on his tiptoes.

"All right, *broom head*," he said. "Now I sweep up the alley with you."

Mangieri struggled to get free and staggered backward, dragging Joe with him. He tripped and slammed into the wall, Joe falling on top of him. Mangieri lay slumped against the wall. As Joe stood up he heard an ambulance siren stop wailing. The ambulance must have come to pick up the man injured in the tornado.

"He's out," Don said.

Joe rubbed his stomach. He fired an angry glare at Don. "Where were you? Why didn't you help?"

Don held up his hands in innocence. "Hey, man, you said you wanted to take care of this."

"You okay, Joe?" Frank shouted, running down the alley.

Mangieri groaned, and Frank looked down at the thug.

"Joe's just fine," Don answered. "But Mangieri's going to have a pretty bad headache for a while."

"Liz told me what happened while I was in the van," Frank explained. "I had Callie call the police."

"Were you able to reach a ham operator?" Joe asked, still holding his stomach.

"Yeah. Got one in Hoboken. He said he'd call Dad's hotel and tell him and Mom we're okay and so is the house."

"Let's get Mangieri to your van and wait for the cops," Don suggested.

Frank and Don helped Mangieri to stand. Mangieri wobbled and nearly fell over, and they had to hold him up as they walked back to the van.

Officer Con Riley and his partner were waiting when they returned to the Hardys' black van. Callie and Chet were gone.

"I see you didn't need any help catching the suspect," Officer Riley said with a smile, pushing his hat back on his head.

"Where are Callie and Chet?" Frank asked Liz.

"Callie wanted to get her tape to WBAY for editing in time for tonight's news," Liz answered. "Chet went with her after the ambulance left with that injured guy."

"You guys know Officer Stewart, don't you?" Officer Riley asked, pointing a thumb at the young policeman standing next to him.

"Sure," Frank said, recognizing the distinctive

white blond hair of Stewart. "You used to walk the beat at city hall, didn't you?"

"That's right," Stewart replied with a smile. "I'll read him his rights, Con."

Mangieri leaned against the police cruiser. "Do you understand these rights as I have read them to you?" Patrolman Stewart concluded moments later.

"Yeah," Mangieri answered weakly.

"He's probably got them memorized," Joe said sarcastically.

Mangieri's black eyes flared with anger. He stared at Joe and addressed Officer Riley. "Hey, Riley, how would you like to be a hero? Save somebody's life?"

"You referring to me, punk?" Joe took a step toward Mangieri.

Officer Riley put his hand on Joe's shoulder. Joe stopped. Stewart then spun Mangieri around to cuff his hands. "What are you talking about?"

"I got some information that could get you a promotion, Riley." Mangieri swiveled his head to face Riley. "Only you got to let me go first."

"You weasel," Joe blurted out.

"What kind of information?" Officer Riley asked.

"Someone's going to get killed." Mangieri was calm.

"Don't believe him, Con," Joe said.

"You're so smart, Hardy," Mangieri said with

a chuckle at Joe. He turned to Officer Riley. "Go ahead. Take me in. Why should I care if someone gets killed."

"Who?" Officer Riley asked.

Mangieri stared at Joe and said bluntly, "Fenton Hardy."

Chapter

2

"WHAT DID YOU SAY?" Joe lurched forward and grabbed Mangieri by the front of his jacket.

Mangieri's smirk quickly melted into fear. Joe held Mangieri up so that they stood nose to nose, the short Mangieri having to stand on tiptoe.

"Listen, you punk, you'd better explain that last remark."

"Easy, Joe." Con placed a strong hand on Joe's shoulder and squeezed.

Joe reluctantly let loose of Mangieri.

"Why do you want to kill our father?" Frank's brown eyes bore into Mangieri's like drill bits.

Mangieri, his voice high-pitched, said, "That's not what I meant, man. I didn't say I was going to kill your old man. I said that I heard someone was out to off him."

15

"Who?" Frank asked.

Mangieri's black eyes narrowed. "You want information, Hardy? Dial four-one-one."

"You slug!" Joe jumped at Mangieri again.

"All right, Joe!" Officer Stewart shouted and pulled Joe back.

Joe jerked free and stared at Mangieri.

"He's lying," Frank said.

Mangieri tried to avoid the cold, rock-hard stares of the Hardys. He slipped into the cruiser through the door Officer Riley was holding open. "Man, how do you know I'm lying?" he shouted from inside the car.

"Your lips are moving," Joe replied without missing a beat.

Mangieri looked like a caged animal. He pressed up against the door and stared straight ahead.

Suddenly he turned his head to Joe. "Forget it, man," he said with a laugh. "I don't say nothing until I see a lawyer. Then I see what kind of a deal I can cut."

Frank looked at Riley and started to ask, "Do you think—"

"Sorry, Frank," Riley interrupted. "This is out of my hands. He's asked for his lawyer. The only thing I can do is finish processing the arrest."

"Don't you believe him about someone out to kill Mr. Hardy?" Don asked.

"That's not the point," Riley said.

"What *is* the point?" Joe took a step toward

Officer Riley. "This creep made a threat against my dad."

Riley's face tightened into an angry expression. The police veteran straightened to his full height and returned Joe's steely stare.

"Your father's the best friend this police department has, and if someone's threatening his life, we'll take care of him." He took a deep breath, and his face relaxed. "Besides, Mangieri's been known to try to lie his way out of jail before. He's probably just bluffing." He looked at Frank. "You two take it easy until we get the truth out of him."

"Yes, sir," Frank said. He tapped Joe on the shoulder and nodded toward the van. Joe backed away from the cruiser, his eyes steady on Mangieri in the backseat.

Officer Riley slammed the back door shut, jumped into the front seat, waited for Stewart to get into the car, and pulled away from the group.

"What are you going to do?" Liz asked.

"Go to the police station to find out if Mangieri's telling the truth," Frank replied as he hopped into the van. Joe planted himself in the driver's seat.

"Call us if you need any help," Don said as he slipped an arm around Liz, and the two of them headed back to help with the tornado cleanup.

"Thanks," Joe said, his voice hard and distant.

Minutes later the boys walked into the officers' lounge of the Bayport Police Department. Frank threw himself into a chair and stared at his brother.

Con Riley was probably right, Mangieri's threat was only a lie, a diversion to get him out of jail. On the other hand, Joe had made sense: they couldn't take the chance that Mangieri was bluffing. All three Hardys— father and sons—had made plenty of enemies while investigating crimes.

"You think he's telling the truth?" They were the first words Joe had spoken since arriving at the station.

"I doubt it," Frank said with a shrug. "How would a greaseball like him get information about someone out to kill Dad?"

Joe stared straight ahead. Frank leaned back in the blue plastic chair and locked his hands behind his head. He knew Joe's anger had reached its combustion point and was now smoldering.

"We've got to let the police do their job," Frank said. Joe turned to meet his brother's hard stare with one of his own but said nothing. "Riley'll let us know if Mangieri is telling the truth or not," Frank added.

"They'd better find something out—and soon!" Joe crumpled the wrapper of the candy bar he'd been eating and tossed it into a corner wastebasket. He was tired and worried.

"Soon" stretched into a half-hour and then an hour. Joe tried several times to find out what Mangieri was telling Riley and the assistant district attorney, but all he got was a chilly warning from the desk sergeant that he and Frank would be thrown out of the police station if Joe didn't stop bothering him. He told the boys that the force was stretched thin due to the tornado. He said they should consider themselves lucky that Con was taking the time to question Mangieri then.

Frank mentally reviewed some of Fenton Hardy's most dangerous cases. Many crooks threatened the police officers who had arrested them or the district attorney who put them in jail or the private eye who tracked them down. Therefore, Frank knew that their father had received his share of threats.

"It's been two hours!" Joe all but shouted as he looked up at the clock on the wall. "You'd think they'd have found out something by now."

"We have."

Joe spun around. Officer Riley stood in the doorway, and he looked exhausted and worried. He motioned for the brothers to follow him. Frank and Joe were at his heels as he led them down the hallway past the interrogation room and into a viewing room.

"Where's Officer Stewart?" Frank asked.

"He asked for some time off," Riley said. "He's worked two straight shifts."

The viewing room looked into the interrogation room through a one-way mirror. The Hardys could see Mangieri sitting alone, smoking a cigarette, his hands uncuffed.

"What's going on?" Joe demanded. "Isn't he under arrest?"

"For now," Officer Riley replied. "How well do you two know Mangieri?" His voice sounded as exhausted as he looked.

"He was kicked out of school," Frank said. "Why?"

"Either of you ever hear of Leonard Mock?"

Frank and Joe glanced at each other and shrugged.

"Mangieri has." Riley turned and stared into the interrogation room.

"So?" Joe stepped up to the one-way mirror and stood next to Riley. "What's the big deal?"

Riley rubbed his eyes. "I was a rookie cop about the time your father resigned from the New York Police Department and started P.I. work here in Bayport. One of the first cases he helped the Bayport police solve involved a con man named Leonard Mock."

Frank's eyes suddenly lit up as he remembered why Mock's name sounded familiar. "He was selling shares in a dummy corporation that was supposed to build a theme park outside of Bayport."

"Correct," Riley said.

"But he's serving a life sentence for murder." Riley didn't reply. He only sighed. Frank shifted uncomfortably. "Isn't he?" he quietly demanded.

Riley locked eyes with Frank. "He was."

"Murder?" Joe spouted.

Riley moved to a table across the room and sat

on the edge. "When the police caught on to Mock's scam, Mock went into hiding. Your father was hired by a group of the investors, and he was able to locate Mock. When we started to arrest him, Mock tried to escape, shots were fired, and my partner was killed."

"Wait a minute," Frank said, his forehead wrinkled in confusion. "What do you mean 'was' serving a life sentence? He's been paroled?"

"I thought the mandatory sentence for a cop killer was life without parole," Joe said.

"It is. But Mock's attorney has somehow gotten the sentence commuted, and—"

"Mock's out of prison," Frank said, finishing Riley's sentence. The police veteran nodded silently.

"This Mock creep is on the streets after killing a cop? I can't believe it!" Joe thrust his hands into his pockets. "What's that got to do with Mangieri threatening Dad?"

Riley rubbed his eyes. "Mangieri says that Mock is trying to hire a gun, someone to kill your father."

"And Mangieri's been hired to—" Joe's voice rose in anger and he was unable to finish his sentence. He headed for the viewing room door. "That creep's not going anywhere."

"It's not Mangieri!" Riley shouted as Joe threw open the door.

Joe stopped in the doorway and slowly turned around. "Who?" he asked through clenched teeth.

For the first time since he could remember,

Frank thought he saw defeat on Riley's face. "We don't know."

Frank was quiet.

"What's your idea, Frank?" Riley asked, knowing Frank's silences meant he was thinking at computer speed.

"My dad's file on the case is full of letters from Mock threatening to kill him if he ever got out of prison."

"He threatened your father in open court while Fenton was testifying against him," Riley added.

"What if Mock is spreading a rumor about hiring a hit man to lead the police in the wrong direction? What if Mock is the killer himself?" Frank reasoned out loud.

"Why would Mangieri rat on Mock?" Joe asked.

"Mangieri would sell out his grandmother if he thought it would be to his advantage," Riley replied.

"Mangieri must know where Mock is hiding out," Frank said, almost to himself.

Riley cleared his throat. He hesitated, then said, "*We* know where Mock is." He paused again. "Mock checked in with a parole officer two days ago."

"And no one told you?" Joe asked, his voice angry.

"Paperwork takes awhile to get around, Joe. Besides, we've all been busy today with the tornado." Riley stood. "Where's your father now?"

"In Philadelphia," Frank answered.

"Good."

"Where's Mock?" Joe asked.

Riley's eyebrows lifted in a knowing glance. "Forget it, Joe. A squad car's been sent to pick up Mock. And Chief Collig has ordered me to tell you two to stay away from Mock. We've got things under control." Riley glanced at his watch.

Frank glanced at Joe and nodded at the door. Joe returned the silent signal.

"We'll try to call our dad in Philadelphia," Frank said, heading for the door.

"Good idea," Riley said behind them.

"Yeah," Joe added. "We'll stay around the house in case Dad decides to come back early."

Frank glanced back at Officer Riley just before he stepped through the doorway. It wouldn't be the first time that he and Joe had disobeyed police orders to stay out of a case.

"Where to?" Joe asked after they had hopped into the van and pulled away from the police station.

"If Mock's been released," Frank began, "then he'd have to check into a halfway house for felons until he can find a job and get settled."

"That rehabilitation place on Fulton Street?"

"Right."

"Suppose the police have already picked him up?"

"Then we'll just look around," Frank replied with a knowing smile.

Joe nodded and stomped on the accelerator. The van lurched forward.

Minutes later Joe's enthusiasm turned into a low groan as he pulled the van up in front of what was left of the Bayport Rehabilitation Center. The freak summer tornado had torn parts of the roof off the building and demolished the left wing.

"He's definitely not here now," Frank announced, just as disappointed as Joe.

They climbed out of the van and stared at the wrecked building.

"Let's see what we can find out, anyway," Frank suggested.

They took in the street with two quick glances before running into the building. Clothes and papers and books and debris had been chucked about by the unforgiving twister's violent winds. Puddles of water stood inches deep up and down the hallway and gave the place a musky, moldy stench already.

"Smells like chemistry class," Frank said, wrinkling his nose.

Although it was early afternoon outside, it was very cloudy and the inside of the building was dark. Frank and Joe pulled out their pocket flashlights and flicked them on.

Frank pointed to his right. "You take that room, and I'll search the office—see if I can find out where Mock's room was."

Joe's reply was a quick jog across the hall and

into the dark room. He moved his small flashlight around the room slowly, the shadows rising and falling like dark targets at a shooting gallery. The room was full of sheets, blankets, pillows, pillow-cases, and towels, all thrown about.

"Just a storage room!" Joe yelled across the hallway as he stepped out of the room. "I'm going to check the rooms down the hall." He started off, not waiting for Frank's answer.

Joe was halfway down the hall when he heard Frank yell out. Without hesitating, he spun around and darted back toward the office, splash-ing pools of water against the walls, his flash-light a tiny beacon bobbing and skipping in front of him.

He tried to stop as he reached the door, but slid on the wet floor and had to grab the door frame to keep himself upright. Joe stared into the coal black room. Frank's light should have been on.

"Frank!" Joe yelled into the room.

Joe heard a scuffling sound of people strug-gling. Then there was a fleshly slap and finally a low, deep moan.

"Frank!"

Joe adjusted the lens on the small flashlight so that it made a larger circle. Then he stepped into the room.

The office was as littered as the storage room. Joe swept the circle of light from his left to his right, slowly moving the telltale beam across overturned desks, chairs, file cabinets, and piles of wet and crumpled files.

Another deep moan caused him to jump, and he flipped the beam to his far right.

Frank lay on the floor holding his left side, his face twisted in pain.

A pale and gaunt man stood over Frank, a broken section of a board gripped in his hands like a club. Several rusted and twisted nails poked out of the end of the board.

"Time to die," the man wheezed. He brought the board down in a deadly arc toward Frank's head.

Chapter

3

FRANK'S EYES WIDENED in horror as he watched the board with the nails arcing down toward him. At the last possible second he rolled to his right, pain shooting through his left side like tiny needles. The board slammed down inches from his chest, the nails sinking into the floor.

"*Aaargh!*" the man screamed as the broken board splintered in his hands.

Joe dropped his flashlight and lunged at the gaunt figure. The two hurtled backward and crashed on top of a desk. A sickening gasp erupted from the stranger, and Joe knew that the breath had been knocked out of him. The room was as silent then as it was dark.

"Joe? You okay?" Frank asked in a forced, strained whisper.

"Yes." Joe stood. "I dropped my flashlight."

"I've got mine." A light flickered on. Frank stood and trained the beam on his attacker.

The man groaned and threw his arms over his face as the beam hit his eyes.

Joe reached down and pulled the man to his feet. He was surprised at how light the man was.

"Let's get him outside," Frank said.

Joe gave the man a slight nudge forward.

"Easy," the man said with a groan.

Guided by the beam of Frank's flashlight, Joe forced the man ahead of him.

Outside, he spun the man around. "All right, mister. Why did you attack—" Joe's sentence ended in a gasp. The man's appearance startled him, and he took a step backward.

The man was as tall as Joe, but he was too thin for his height. Can't be more than one hundred thirty-five pounds, Joe thought.

What stunned Joe the most was the man's face. His skin was tight against his skull and cheekbones, and small red sores stood out in contrast to the sickly yellow-white of his skin. The man's light blue eyes, which seemed to be covered with a milky substance, stared out at Joe from deep, dark sockets.

Joe had seen the look before, but only on dead men.

The man sucked in a deep breath through yellow clenched teeth.

"Ssssooo, Hardyssss," the man hissed. Then he coughed, deep hacking explosions that reminded Joe of metal being twisted and torn.

"Who are you?" Frank asked. "Why did you attack us?"

The man smiled, his thin blue lips pulling across his face in triumph. He opened his mouth to speak but doubled over in another coughing spasm. This time he fell to his knees. Frank reached down to help the man.

"Get—away—from—me," the man forced out through dry coughs.

"He was probably just looking for someplace to stay. Maybe he doesn't have a home," Joe said. "I'll call an ambulance on the CB." Joe ran to the van.

Why would a homeless person be hanging around the rehab center? Frank asked himself. Better yet, how would some stranger know our last name?

The man's coughing increased, and he fell flat on the ground.

Frank knelt beside him. "How can I help you?" he pleaded. "Joe, hurry!"

The man must have some ID, Frank thought. He reached into the man's front shirt pocket, but his hand was instantly smacked away.

"You—want—to—help—me?" the man wheezed. "Then—*die*, Frank Hardy!"

29

"What?" Frank wasn't sure he had heard the man correctly.

"An ambulance is on its way," Joe said, rejoining Frank. He stared down at the man. "How is he?"

"Delirious. I think he just told me to die."

"That'ssss—right." The man's coughing had stopped, and he was now breathing sporadically in screeching gasps.

Joe knelt on one knee. "Who are you?"

"Leonard Mock." The man swallowed hard.

"Mock?" Joe glanced at his brother and then back down at the pale figure of Leonard Mock. "What are you doing here? The police—"

"Came by the rehab center and went," Mock interrupted. "They couldn't find me, just like before."

"Before?" Frank was puzzled. "Before what?"

"Just like before. The first time. The first ti—" Again Mock succumbed to a fit of dry, hacking coughs.

"What are you doing here in Bayport?" Joe asked once Mock had stopped.

"Waiting for Fenton Hardy." Mock's hollow, dead eyes flicked from Frank to Joe. "But you two will do. You'll do just fine."

Frank knew they had very little time. Once the ambulance arrived, the police would take over and the Hardys would be forbidden to question Mock.

"You've come back to Bayport to kill Fenton Hardy," Frank stated.

The man attempted a laugh but only coughed. "No," he finally gasped.

"Then why?" Joe asked, anger replacing his impatience.

"I—came—to die," Mock announced.

"What?" Joe blasted back.

Mock swallowed and the grimace on his face and shudder of his body told Frank that the man's pain ran deep and hard.

"Cancer," Mock forced out.

"That's why they commuted your sentence," Frank said.

Mock turned to Frank and smiled. "You're the smart one, aren't you? The governor couldn't keep a dying man in prison. It's inhuman." Mock's head jerked back as he bellowed a laugh; the laugh was replaced by a deep, bone-jarring gasp that Frank thought would be the man's last breath.

"If you didn't plan on killing our father, why did you come back here? Why did you attack Frank?" Joe demanded.

"You startled me. I thought you were looters."

"How do you know who we are?" Joe continued.

"I know all about Fenton Hardy and his famous detective sons. Like father, like sons, huh?" Mock smacked his dry lips. "I subscribed to the local hometown paper. Couldn't miss an exciting issue.''

"Do you know Martin Mangieri?" Frank asked.

"No." Mock's voice was suddenly weak and soft.

"He's a two-bit crook who says he's got street news that you plan to kill our father."

"*Had* planned," Mock replied, his eyes widening. Then more softly he repeated, "Had planned. Your old man sent me to prison for life. I wanted him dead. Then I got cancer."

Mock closed his eyes and swallowed. Again his body shook, and he clenched his teeth against the pain.

Thunder rumbled low and deep in the distance. The faint shrill of the ambulance's siren could be heard several blocks away.

Frank knew they had little time left. "You mean that you don't blame our father for cracking the case against you?"

"Want to hear a little joke?" Mock replied. "The closer you get to death, the more you think about life. Real funny, huh? Well, I've made peace with my hate and anger."

"Good," Joe said with a sigh. He suddenly felt sorry for the man. "Can we help you? Can we do anything for you?"

Mock let out a screeching laugh that stunned the Hardys.

"You fools," Mock groaned. "I've only said

that I've made my peace with *myself*, not with your father. I may not kill him, but I still want him dead!''

Joe reached out to grab the man, but Frank knocked his younger brother's hand away.

"You want to hit me, don't you, Joe Hardy? You want to do something to hurt me. Now multiply that hatred by a lifetime sentence, and you'll have a little taste of the hatred that has eaten at me."

"Why?" Frank fired back. "Why do you want our father dead?" The ambulance was getting closer.

Mock's light blue eyes widened. "I rotted in that prison for years. Can you understand that? Fenton Hardy was free. Free to see his two sons grow up." Mock closed his eyes and swallowed. "To see his sons grow up. My son—my own son—"

Mock gasped and then choked, trying to suck in air.

The ambulance screamed to a stop. The thunder clapped closer and louder.

Mock inhaled. He opened his eyes and stared at the Hardys, a vision of death in his milky blue eyes. An evil smile spread across his yellow-white face.

"My own son," he began, softly, slowly, "will finish what *his* father could not. What goes around comes around."

The ambulance attendants jumped from the vehicle. Mock sank back. Frank was afraid the dying man had lost consciousness. He grabbed Mock by his shirt lapels and pulled him up.

"What about your son?" Frank asked desperately.

"Everything comes full circle. Fenton Hardy put me in prison. *Killed me!* Now my son will kill Fenton Hardy!"

Chapter

4

"YOU TWO WERE SUPPOSED to stay off this case, remember?" an angry Con Riley was saying through clenched teeth as the ambulance pulled away.

"We just wanted to look around, see if we could find anything that could help the police." Frank was trying to be tactful.

"Sure," shot back a doubtful Officer Riley. "What did you expect to find?"

"We didn't expect to find Leonard Mock," Joe answered quickly as his eyes followed the ambulance up the street.

Mock had barely spoken about his son killing Fenton Hardy when he had collapsed. Frank and Joe had watched as paramedics put the dying man on a respirator and then loaded him into the ambulance. Frank had asked about Mock recovering.

The paramedic in the back of the ambulance shrugged.

"What will happen to Mock?" Joe asked.

"He'll be in intensive care at Bayport General Hospital."

"Under guard," Frank added.

Riley's eyes were bloodshot and were staring past the Hardys. The police veteran said in a tired voice, "Yeah."

"It's not Mock I'm worried about," Frank said. "It's his son."

"Why?" Riley asked.

Joe explained about Mock's son, shaking his head.

Frank's forehead wrinkled in thought. He studied the devastated rehab center. "Why did Mock come back to the rehab center?"

"What are you driving at, Frank?" Officer Riley asked.

"Mock came back to the rehab center for something," Frank announced.

"In his room!" Joe shouted.

The Hardys started for the front door of the building.

"Wait a minute!"

Frank and Joe stopped and turned to face a tired and angry Con Riley.

"You two have been told more than once to stay off this case," the police veteran said firmly.

"We're not going to stand around while someone goes after our father," Joe responded just as firmly. "You don't understand—"

"I understand perfectly!"

Frank was stunned by the force and anger in Officer Riley's voice. He had known the police veteran since childhood but had never seen Con Riley shake with anger.

"Remember, Joe," Frank began softly, "Mock killed Officer Riley's partner."

Joe's face flushed with embarrassment. "I'm sorry."

Officer Riley shifted uncomfortably. "Forget it. The thing we've got to do is find out if Mock's son is in Bayport."

"Dad's old files might help," Frank suggested.

"That's a good place to start," Riley said. He headed for the building, stopped, and turned. "I understand why you two want to help. Chief Collig will probably have my badge for this, but if you promise to keep a low profile, I'll let you help."

Frank and Joe looked at each other, smiled, and followed Officer Riley into the building.

Mock's room was located in the one wing that had survived the tornado—even the roof was intact. Without electricity, they had to use flashlights, and the search was slow.

The sky rumbled, lightning flashed, and then a heavy rain fell.

Frank began searching in a chest of drawers. He

didn't like the rain or the slow pace of the search. He became angry as each drawer revealed nothing.

Mock had returned for something, but what? Obviously, Mock had kept in touch with someone in Bayport, or else how would he have known Frank and Joe well enough to recognize them on sight?

"Frank, look at this."

In the dim light from his flashlight Frank watched as Joe stood just outside the small closet, unwrapping a paper bundle. Inside were newsclippings about the Hardys and some of their cases, faded newspaper photos, and several photographs.

"He wasn't kidding when he said he kept tabs on us," Joe said.

"Not only us," Frank added, 'but our friends as well." Frank flipped through the photos: Frank, Joe, and Callie at the beach; Chet and Joe playing football; Frank and Joe eating at Mr. Pizza; Frank and Callie coming out of a movie theater.

"Surveillance photos," Joe said without emotion.

"Looks that way," Con said. "Someone's been watching you and keeping Mock informed."

"Who?" Joe asked.

"Mock's son," Frank replied. "But he hasn't been watching us for long."

"How can you tell?" Officer Riley asked.

"Look at the picture with Callie and me coming out of the theater. See the title of the movie?"

Joe nodded.

"The Majestic was showing that about eight months ago," Frank said.

Officer Riley took the photos from Frank and glanced through them. A smaller photo fell to the floor.

"What's that?" Joe asked.

Riley picked up the photo, studied it for a moment, then answered, "Looks like a school photo." He turned it over and read, " 'Bobby—Kindergarten.' The date's smudged, though." He handed the photo to Frank. "Recognize the boy?"

Frank looked at the photo. "He does look a little familiar, but I can't place him," he said after a moment. "The photo's old, though. Look at the shirt." He turned the photo so Joe could get a better look. "That style went out when we were kids."

Joe took the photo from Frank and stared. "He does look like somebody I know, but who I can't say."

"It's probably Mock's son, but why only a kindergarten photo? Why not other school pictures?" Frank took back the picture and flipped through the whole bundle one more time.

"Chief Collig will need to know about this," Officer Riley said. He cleared his throat and reached for the bundle. "I'll have to take those, Frank."

Frank hesitated, then palmed the kindergarten photo before handing the bundle to Officer Riley.

They walked out into the rain.

"I'll make sure our best detectives get on this," Officer Riley said as he opened the door of his police cruiser. "Try to contact your father and let him know what's going on."

"Right," Frank said, scrunching up his shoulders against the cold rain. "Our car phone's out, but we've got a CB that can reach a ham operator."

"Good." Officer Riley slid into his cruiser and fired up the engine. He stared straight ahead and said, "This kid of Mock's who's gunning for your father may also be looking for you two. I suggest you find a place to lay low for a while." He looked up at the Hardys, smiled slightly, then shut his door and sped away.

"What now?" Joe asked as he and Frank hopped into the van.

"First we need to figure out exactly who this is." Frank held up the kindergarten photo of Bobby Mock.

"Officer Riley's going to be upset with you," Joe said.

"It won't be the first time," Frank replied. "Or probably the last."

The Hardys' CB buzzed and clicked.

"Number One Girl calling Sherlock. Over," Callie said over the radio.

Frank sighed. Callie liked to use handles—trucker slang for nicknames. She had dubbed Frank "Sherlock," Joe "Bone Crusher," Chet "Pizza King," and herself "Number One Girl." It could have been worse, Frank thought.

Frank grabbed the handset. "What is it, Callie? Over."

"Number One Girl," Callie insisted.

"Okay, Number One Girl. What is it?" Frank glanced at Joe, who was laughing at Frank.

"Go to the *Times*, Sherlock. The Paper Girl's got something you ought to see."

"Paper Girl?"

"Liz!"

"Oh."

Joe laughed louder.

Frank ignored Joe. "Where are you, Callie?"

"I wish you'd use my handle, Sherlock." Callie paused, and Frank knew she was angry. "Pizza King and I are still at WBAY."

"How's Chet's finger?" Joe asked.

"Cal—I mean, Number One Girl, Joe wants to know about Pizza King's finger."

"He's got a splint on it, but it's really only bruised. Paper Girl is at the Bayport *Times* and has something she wants to show you."

"She say what it was?"

"No. She refused to say."

"Okay, Number One Girl," Frank said. "Will I see you later?"

"If you're lucky," Callie said. "Over."

"Over," Frank said. He hung up the handset and shot a glance at Joe. "What's so funny?"

Joe forced himself not to laugh while he said, "Ah, what fools we make out of ourselves for true love."

"Just drive, *Bone Crusher.*"

Minutes later Frank and Joe were at the Bayport *Times,* listening to Liz Webling as she sat behind her desk. Don sat on one corner of the desk.

"I've been working as a stringer for some time," Liz was saying. Joe shot her a questioning glance.

"A part-time reporter," Don answered.

Joe locked eyes with Don. He had asked Liz not Don.

"That's why I have access to the morgue," Liz continued.

"The morgue?" Joe asked.

"It's what they call the file room where they keep the 'dead' issues," Don explained. "Get it?"

Joe locked eyes with Don again. Something about Don didn't sit right with Joe, but he couldn't put his finger on it—not yet, anyway.

"Another reporter heard about what Mangieri told the assistant district attorney and Riley. He managed to get his hands on the parole report on Leonard Mock."

"We've already found Mock, and it's not him we're worried about," Joe said impatiently.

"It's his son," Liz announced, leaning back in her chair and locking her hands behind her head.

"How did you know that?" Frank asked.

"I'm a reporter."

Liz leaned forward and stared intensely at Frank. Frank forced himself not to smile. He could tell Liz was enjoying playing the part of detective.

"Shortly after the trial," Liz began, "Mock lost custody of his son, and Bobby Mock was adopted by another family."

"What about Bobby's mother?" Frank asked.

"She died when Bobby was only three," Don answered.

Joe was about to ask Don how he knew that when Frank said, "If Bobby Mock was adopted, then his name would have been changed and that could be why we don't know anybody named Mock at school."

"That's right," Joe said, suddenly excited. "All we have to do now is find out who adopted Bobby Mock."

"Forget it," Don said.

"What?" Joe didn't like Don butting in, answering all the questions, and he didn't like Don's know-it-all tone.

"Adoption records are held by the vital records section of city hall," Don explained, sounding bored. "The only way vital records will let you look at adoption papers is through a court order. And trying to get a judge to unseal adoption records is like trying to get Joe to give out his book of phone numbers."

"How do you know so much about it?" Joe fired back, ignoring Don's jab at his numerous girlfriends.

"His dad is city manager," Liz reminded the Hardys.

"That's right," Don said smugly. "And while you two can't get to the records, I can."

"How?" Frank asked quickly. Frank could tell Joe was getting angrier by the moment. Joe didn't like interference, even helpful interference. Or was Joe jealous of Don because of Liz?

"I know everybody at city hall. Nobody's going to question my hanging around, especially during a crisis. I told you guys earlier I wanted in on this case."

"You're in," Frank said. Joe shot Frank an angry look. "And thanks."

"No problem." Don jumped up from the desk. "I'd better start now." He left the newsroom and disappeared down the hallway.

"We'd better start, too," Joe said, not wanting Don to get too far ahead of them.

"We owe you one," Frank said to Liz as they headed out of the newsroom.

"Forget it, Frank. On second thought, let me have the exclusive on this story, and we'll call it even."

"You've got it."

Once outside, Joe darted through the rain at a jog.

"Hey, what's your hurry?" Frank asked.

"You don't think I'm going to let Don solve this case before we do, do you?"

That confirms it, Frank thought, Joe *is* jealous of Don. With all the girls in Bayport Joe could impress, he had to decide to try to impress Liz Webling, the one girl who wouldn't have anything to do with him.

A roar split the air. It sounded like thunder, but Frank knew no thunder would crease his left temple with a searing hot wind. Shards of brick flew off the *Times* building where the bullet finally hit and exploded. A three-inch chunk of brick slammed into the back of Frank's head.

He fell to the wet pavement.

"Frank!" Joe shouted. He ran to his brother.

Blackness swam in front of Frank's eyes, slowly falling like a curtain over his brain. He tried to push himself up but couldn't. Time seemed to slow down. Frank raised his head and saw a man in a black raincoat and ski mask standing in the alley across the street. His hands were coiled around a .357 automatic, its deadly barrel trained on the Hardys.

The man fired again. Joe Hardy fell next to his brother.

Chapter

5

FRANK FOUGHT AGAINST the unconsciousness that sought to drown him. Through a red haze he watched as the black-clad man retreated into the darkness of the alley and disappeared.

He tried to push himself up again, but again he fell back to the wet pavement.

"Frank!" he heard someone yell in the distance.

His name echoed throughout his head, followed by a pounding that felt as though something were trying to push its way out through his temples.

He felt hands on his arm, turning him over. Once on his back, he looked up into the gray-black sky. Slowly the image of his brother came into focus.

"Joe," Frank said weakly. "I thought you were shot."

"Played possum," Joe said. "You okay?"

"Yeah, I guess." Frank sat up. "If you call an eighteen-wheel truck driving through your head okay." With Joe's help, Frank stood on wobbly legs. He had to lean against the brick building to steady himself.

"Not a truck," Joe said, fingering the three-inch hole the bullet had left in the brick wall.

"Automatic," Frank said, looking at the hole. "Three-fifty-seven."

"Frank! Joe! You okay?" Liz ran from the building, her face showing worry and fear. Several other employees were with her.

"Yeah," Frank said, trying to stand to his full height. He rocked back and forth as dizziness washed over him.

"What happened?" Liz asked.

"We don't know," Joe answered quickly. "I think I ought to treat that bump," he said to Frank. "And I think we have to get in out of the rain."

"Yeah," Frank replied.

"Everything's okay," Joe said to the small crowd that had formed around them. "Just a little accident." As the others headed back inside, Joe said to Liz, "I need to talk to you, Liz."

Once in the back of the van Joe got out the first-aid kit and began applying iodine to the back of Frank's head.

"Owww!" Frank shouted. He glared at Joe,

who only smiled. "You don't have to enjoy this."

"What happened?" Liz asked again.

"We were shot at," Joe began.

"Bobby Mock, we think," Frank interrupted.

"How can you be sure?" Liz asked. "According to my sources, Leonard Mock said that Bobby is supposed to kill *your father*. Not you."

"We're the next best targets," Frank said as Joe finished up and put the first-aid kit away.

"I think the police ought to know about this," Liz said as she started to open the door.

"Wait," Frank said. He made a grab for her but fell back. "Man, I'm going to have some headache."

Joe hopped out into the clean dry air. The rain had finally let up. Joe gently grabbed Liz's arm to turn her around.

He began softly. "Look, Liz, Chief Collig has already threatened to throw us in jail for interfering with the investigation. If he knows about this, he'll put us in protective custody, and we won't be able to help find this Bobby Mock before he tries to kill our father."

"I don't know," Liz said hesitantly.

"Please, Liz. For me." Joe flashed his best smile at Liz and tried to look slightly helpless to appeal to her sympathies.

Liz crossed her arms. "You don't have to try to charm me, Joe Hardy." She stared for a few moments into Joe's eyes. "Okay. If it'll help, I won't say anything."

"Trying to steal my girl again, Hardy?"

Joe and Liz turned as Don walked up to the trio, his hands in his pockets.

Joe flushed with anger and embarrassment. "No."

Don looked into the van. "Hey, Frank. What are you doing in there?"

"Just getting ready to leave," Frank replied, gently stepping down from the van. "Find out anything?"

"No," Don replied with a shrug. "The computers were down. I'll have to go through the files by hand. That's why I came back here. I need to know roughly when Bobby Mock was adopted."

"I'll get it," Liz said and dashed into the newspaper building.

Don turned back to the Hardys. "As soon as I locate the file, I'll copy it and give it to you."

"You'll get into a lot of trouble if your father finds out," Frank said.

"No problem. I'd hate to think what it would be like to lose my father." Don's voice was distant, distracted.

Frank looked at Joe. "We need to get home."

"Why are you going there?" Don's question was more demanding than curious.

"Just an idea," Frank replied, purposely being evasive. "Let's go, Joe."

"I'll drop by later with the file," Don said as the Hardys hopped into the van.

"What's this idea you have?" Joe asked minutes later.

"Turn here," Frank said in reply.

"Where are we going?"

"Bayport Electronics. To find out who this is." Frank held up the kindergarten photo of Bobby Mock.

"How?"

"I read an article a few months ago about a new computer program that can age the people in photos like this one. You get a computer-generated image of what the person should look like at any age."

"I saw that on the news. They use it to help find runaways or kids who have been kidnapped." They rode on in silence a few minutes. Then Joe finally asked, "So, how old do you think Bobby Mock is now?"

"Leonard Mock's only a couple years older than Dad." Frank stared at the photo. "And judging by Bobby's shirt, I'd say he's somewhere between fifteen and twenty."

"That's quite a spread."

"It's the best we have so far."

"How long will this take?"

"An hour, two at the most."

"I'm going to the hospital," Joe announced. He steered the van into the oval drive of Bayport

Electronics. "Bobby may get wind that his old man's there and try to visit him."

"I'll meet you there after the photo is done."

Joe waited until Frank entered the BE building and then drove away. He didn't really like the idea of splitting up, especially now that Mock's son had made his first move, but time was a luxury the Hardys could not afford.

"I'm sorry, Joe," said Officer Bill Murphy, "but Chief Collig will bust me back down to traffic control if I let you in there."

Joe and Officer Murphy stood at the nurses' station only a few yards away from the intensive care unit where Leonard Mock was clinging to life with the help of a life-support machine.

"I only want to talk to him," Joe pleaded.

"Nope." The young cop was unmoved. "The suspect is unconscious anyway. The doctors say he may not even make it through the night."

"Okay," Joe said. "But you can't keep me from waiting."

"No, I can't," Officer Murphy said, his thumbs tucked into his gun belt. "But I can tell you where to wait." He pointed behind Joe. "In the lobby."

"Humph!" Joe shook his head and headed back to the fifth-floor lobby. He was afraid that if he caused any trouble, Officer Murphy would have him escorted from the hospital.

Joe thrust his hands into his pockets and walked

slowly toward the lobby. He glanced over his shoulder. Officer Murphy was leaning against the nurses' station, talking to a young blond nurse. An idea flashed through Joe's mind: If Murphy could be distracted long enough, Joe could sneak into Mock's room.

Joe ducked into a closet. Green surgical shirts and pants, gloves, masks, and hair covers lined the shelves. Joe quickly put the hospital garb on over his clothes, finally covering his face with a surgical mask.

He opened the closet door and glanced down the corridor. Officer Murphy was still engaged in a lively conversation with the pretty blond nurse. Joe stepped into the hallway and walked casually toward the nurses' station.

He grabbed a clipboard from a nearby desk and pretended to be looking at it while he passed Officer Murphy and the nurse.

He held his breath as he neared the door to ICU. He glanced back quickly and saw that neither Officer Murphy nor the nurse had even given him a glance. He pushed the door open and entered the intensive care ward.

The ICU ward was a long hallway with several doors leading off it into individual rooms. Joe checked the names on the doors until he found the one marked "Leonard Mock."

He glanced back down the hallway, took a deep breath, and quietly opened the door.

The room was full of shadows produced by the blinking lights of the life-support equipment. A steady, persistent hum flowed from the machinery. Mock's wheezing breaths sent a chill through Joe. He shuddered and walked quietly over to the bed.

Leonard Mock looked worse than he had at the rehab center. His skin was stretched even tighter against his skull, and his lips were drawn back to reveal large, yellow teeth in a death's head smile. Even though Mock's eyelids were closed over his large, bulging eyes, Joe got the feeling that Leonard Mock was watching his every move. The life-support equipment hummed and beeped, keeping track of the last hours of Leonard Mock.

Joe suddenly thought he should leave and was about to go out into the hall when he heard footsteps moving toward him. He dashed into the bathroom and closed the door, leaving a slit through which he could see the entire room.

The door to the room opened, and Joe watched as a man walked over to Mock's bed and stood for several moments without saying a thing. The man was silhouetted against the lights of the machine, his black outline revealing a dark raincoat.

"Father," the man said, his voice low. He leaned over the bed.

Bobby Mock! Joe took a deep breath.

"The sons—Frank and Joe—are dead! Their friends are next. And when Hardy returns, he'll be dead, too."

Joe stepped from the bathroom. "Over my dead body," he said.

The man swung around. Through the eyeholes of the black ski mask, Joe could see the confused, questioning eyes of Bobby Mock but nothing else.

The man reached inside his raincoat. The gun! Joe thought.

Joe leapt at the man and threw a hard right punch to his left cheek. Then he shoved him against the wall. Joe grabbed the man's hand and held it inside the raincoat. Joe could feel the hard steel outline of the .357 magnum.

Bobby Mock backhanded Joe, knocking him against a life-support machine. A staccato buzzing filled the air. Leonard Mock twitched on his death bed.

Bobby Mock pulled the .357 automatic from beneath his raincoat and pointed it at Joe.

Joe kicked out and got Mock's hand with his toe. The gun flew across the room and hit the floor, exploding as it landed.

Joe lunged at Mock and caught him in the sternum with his shoulder. Pain exploded in Joe's shoulder, and he bounced off Mock. As Joe reached for his shoulder, Mock planted a crushing right on Joe's jaw. Joe staggered backward.

The room swam as Joe tried to regain his senses. He was dazed and breathless. Mock ran for his gun.

The door to the room burst open, and Officer

Murphy flew into the room. "What's going on in here?" he shouted.

Joe turned. He was distracted just long enough for Mock to grab his gun. Mock spun around, striking Joe across the cheek with an upward swing.

Joe crumpled to the floor.

Chapter

6

"IF YOU DON'T GET OUT of my hair and out of my office right now, I'm going to call security and have you thrown out!" yelled a haggard Bruce Smith.

What hair? Frank asked himself as he watched the overhead light bounce off the older man's bald head.

For the past fifteen minutes Frank had been arguing with Smith, trying to convince the president of BE to let him use a computer terminal and the photo aging program.

"I can be in and out of the program in an hour," Frank repeated for the umpteenth time.

"No! I don't have the time or the space for one of your hare-brained schemes, Hardy. The tornado caused our mainframe to dump just about every program we had, and we've got to get our systems back up or lose our government contracts." Smith rubbed his shiny scalp. With clenched teeth he said, "Now, get out of my office and out of BE."

Frank threw his hands up and left. A dead end. He'd have to think of another way to try to identify Mock's son. Perhaps a police artist could help. That would mean asking Chief Collig, and Frank knew the answer already.

He pulled the photo from his pocket and looked at the back. If only the date weren't smudged, then he could be more sure of Bobby Mock's age.

"Hey, Frank!" someone called out just before Frank reached the front glass doors of BE.

Frank turned and saw David Simpson walking up to him. David was vice president of BE and had been out to Bayport High's computer club several times to teach new programing techniques. He had always been impressed with Frank's expertise.

"Hi, David. I hear your computers crunched all your programs."

"Not all, thank goodness, but enough to make me wish I was driving a truck for a living." David pointed at Frank's bandage. "Looks like that tornado just about wiped out your programming, too."

"Yeah, I guess."

"Say, if you're looking for a part-time job, we need temporary programmers until we're completely back on line."

The thought struck Frank, and he almost said yes. What better way to get access to the computer program he needed. Then again, he would probably be assigned to punch in some boring government documentation. That could take hours—time he didn't have to spare.

"Sorry," Frank said with a shrug.

"Well, let me know if you need anything." David turned to leave.

"Wait, there is something." Frank looked at the photo in his hand. "I need to identify this kid."

David took the photo and looked at it. "Working on a case?"

"Yes. Missing person. It's important that I find him as soon as possible."

David looked at the photo again and then at Frank. "The problem is that I won't be able to get to you right away. I had to steal the break I'm on now."

"I understand, but this is a matter of life or death. I've already talked to Mr. Smith, and he—"

"Said no," David interrupted with a knowing smile.

"Right."

"Tell you what. Have you got a modem for your home computer?"

"Only the best," Frank replied, aware of what David was going to say next.

"I'll get to this as soon as I can and send the results via the modem. Let me make a laser print of this for our computer.'' David was gone and back in a matter of minutes. ''Here.'' He handed the small school photo back to Frank.

''Can you tell me about when I might expect it?'' Frank didn't want to sound too anxious, but the sooner they knew who Bobby Mock was, the sooner they could have him in jail.

''Sorry, Frank,'' David replied with a shake of his head.

'Thanks. I'll wait at home.''

''Take it easy, Frank. Say hello to your dad for me.''

''I'll be sure to do that.''

Frank left the Bayport Electronics building. He hoped that Joe had had better luck at the hospital. He flagged down a taxi and headed to Bayport General. He was tired. He sat back in the seat and had to force himself to stay awake. First the freak tornado had nearly torn apart Bayport, and now a killer was out to murder the Hardys. It had not been a good day.

''Ouch!'' Joe moaned as the doctor made sure Joe's shoulder wasn't dislocated. He was sitting on a bench in the emergency room, Chief Collig and Officer Riley hovering over him like angry parents.

''Serves you right for interfering with the police,'' Chief Collig growled. ''I ought to throw the book at you.''

''If I hadn't walked in when I did, you'd never

have known that Mock's son was in the hospital," Joe said.

"He's right, Chief," Officer Riley said in Joe's defense.

Chief Collig scowled at Officer Riley.

"I want Officer Murphy in my office tomorrow morning," Chief Collig ordered.

"Where *is* Officer Murphy?" Joe asked.

"Stationed in front of Mock's door, where he should have been in the first place," Officer Riley replied. "He's got a nasty bruise on his chin where Mock's son slugged him with that magnum, but he'll survive."

"Not when I'm through chewing him out," Chief Collig added.

"There," the doctor said. "You'll be okay, but you're sure you didn't run into the wall and not his chest?"

Joe looked into the young doctor's eyes. "I know the difference between a wall and some guy's chest." He turned to Officer Riley. "I'm telling you his chest was like steel."

"Joe!" Frank shouted as he entered the room.

"Please, don't shout," Joe said as he squeezed his eyelids shut.

"Good. You're both here." Chief Collig began buttoning up his raincoat. "I'm going to tell you two for the last time to keep your noses out of police business. Officer Riley, if you see these two working on this case, I want you to hold them until their parents return from Phila-delphia.''

''Yes, sir,'' Officer Riley said.

Frank bristled at Chief Collig's order. ''On what charge?''

''No charge,'' Chief Collig said as he put his hat on and buttoned up his raincoat. He smiled. ''Protective custody.'' Then he stormed out.

Frank and Joe turned to Officer Riley.

Riley shrugged. ''Sorry, boys. You heard the chief.''

Joe was ready to tell Frank what had happened when a rapid, high-pitched beeping sounded in the hospital corridor.

Frank, Joe, and Officer Riley ran out into the hallway and followed the nurses to Mock's ICU room.

''What happened?'' Officer Riley quickly asked Murphy.

''I—I—I don't know,'' the young officer stammered.

A tall thin doctor was leaning over Leonard Mock. He pulled the sheet over Mock's body and turned to the Hardys.

The doctor's face was grim, but his voice was matter-of-fact. ''He's dead.''

Frank and Joe returned home to find that elec-tricity had been restored, but the phone lines were still down. Frank contacted the ham radio operator in Hoboken and relayed a message to his father that they were all okay. He didn't mention anything about Leonard or Bobby Mock.

Frank and Joe said little as they ate and got ready for bed. The one thought that kept crossing their minds was, How would Bobby Mock react to his father's death?

They decided to set the alarm system to the house after double-checking the windows and doors to make sure they were all locked.

Before going to sleep, Frank made up his mind to visit BE the first thing in the morning to check up on the aging progress of the kindergarten photo of Bobby Mock. With the phone lines still down, the modem was useless.

The next day dawned gray and wet. Frank had risen early to check his father's old files and was chewing on an English muffin when Joe walked into the kitchen.

"So, what's the plan for the day?" Joe asked as he took a mixing bowl down from a cabinet and grabbed a box of cereal.

"The phones are still out, so we'll have to go to BE for the photo of Bobby Mock."

Joe dumped the half-full box of cereal into the bowl and covered the flakes with milk. "Then what?" he asked as he crunched down on the cereal.

"Then we find Bobby Mock and turn him over to the police."

Joe reached behind himself for the orange juice sitting on the cabinet. Only a little juice remained in the bottom of the jug so Joe didn't bother to get a glass. He raised the edge to his lips and drank. The cold, tart juice felt good against his dry throat.

"You know what Aunt Gertrude would say if she saw you doing that?" Frank said with a sly smile.

"What she doesn't know won't hurt me," Joe quipped back.

The phone suddenly rang, and both Frank and Joe nearly jumped out of their chairs.

"I thought you said—" Joe began.

"Must have gotten fixed sometime in the night," Frank said. He was ready to answer the ringing phone when it suddenly stopped and he heard his computer blip on upstairs. He sat back down.

"Aren't you going to see who it is?" Joe asked, referring to the image that was printing right then of Bobby Mock.

"It'll take a few minutes to print." Frank bit down on the last of his muffin and washed it down with a glass of milk. He calmly dusted his hands and then headed for his computer.

Joe finished off his bowl of cereal and then scoured the cabinets for another box, but there was none. He imagined he knew what Old Mother Hubbard's dog felt like. Maybe, they could stop off at a convenience store and get some cinnamon rolls.

Joe walked from the kitchen to the living room and swung around the banister to head upstairs. He stopped short when he saw Frank sitting on the stairs.

"Whoa," Joe said with a smile, but his smile quickly vanished when he saw Frank's face.

Frank was holding the computer printout in his hands, his face was gray, and his eyes were fixed and staring.

"What is it?" Joe asked, his voice almost a whisper. Frank didn't answer. He only stared. "*Who* is it?"

Frank still didn't answer, but this time he slowly raised his hand to give Joe the color printout of eighteen-year-old Bobby Mock.

Joe gasped as he recognized the computer picture of their best friend—Chet Morton!

Chapter

7

"THAT'S IMPOSSIBLE!" Joe shouted.

"I think so, too," Frank said, his voice a whisper. "But that's why we thought he looked so familiar."

"Someone's trying to set Chet up," Joe said.

"And make fools of us. Mock had years to plan this."

"This sounds like something out of a spy novel." Joe sat down on the steps, still staring at the computerized Chet Morton.

"Before you got up this morning, I went down to the basement and got out Dad's oldest files, the stuff he didn't put on computer. Mock's file was full of letters threatening to kill Dad and destroy our family."

"How does this fit?"

"What better way to get even than lead us to believe that our friends are against us? Didn't you say that Bobby Mock promised his father that he would get our friends?"

"Yeah," Joe replied. "That's why he had those pictures of you, me, Callie, and Chet."

"Exactly."

"What now?"

"First, we find Chet and show him this." He pointed to the printout. "From what Bobby Mock said at the hospital last night, we can assume that Chet's life is in danger."

Joe stood up and walked back down to the living room. He put the printout on the coffee table and picked up the phone. He tried the Morton home first, but a telephone company tape recording told him that the phone was out of service. That would make sense. Not all the phones in Bayport would be fixed at the same time.

Frank called Callie to warn her that her life might be in danger. Mr. Shaw told Frank that Callie had gone to the television station. She had tried to call Frank, but their line was busy. Callie must have tried to call while the modem was working.

Frank tried WBAY. Callie had left with a tall, heavyset blond kid, the assignment editor said. The "heavyset blond kid" was probably Chet Morton. What was Chet doing at the television station? Frank asked himself.

The assignment editor went on to explain that Callie wanted to get some shots from the top of the old Farmers and Merchants Bank building in the downtown area. It had seen some of the worst damage.

"Looks like Newshawk Shaw is dragging Chet all over town," Joe said after Frank told him what the assignment editor said.

"We've got to find Chet and warn him—and Callie, too," Frank replied.

"You read my mind."

They were out the door when Don West pulled up in his red sports car. He jumped from his car and ran up to the Hardys.

"You're not going to believe this," he said, almost out of breath. He took a file from under his raincoat and handed it to Frank. "I had to wait until this morning before anybody arrived at work. These are only copies." He held up the folder. "Bobby Mock's adoption papers."

The three went into the house.

Frank opened the file and began reading.

"What happened to your cheek?" Joe asked, noticing a reddish bruise on Don's left cheek.

"Some boxes fell on me when I was trying to find those files," he replied with a shrug, avoiding Joe's eyes.

"I can't believe this!" Frank threw the file on the coffee table.

Joe picked up the file and opened it.

"I couldn't believe it, either," Don said.

"It looks like Chet Morton is Bobby Mock."

"He can't be!" Joe blurted out. "I've known him for years."

"What's that got to do with anything?" Don asked.

"Could anyone have planted this file in vital records?" Frank asked.

"I doubt it," Don replied. "I had to be sneaky just to get copies made without getting caught."

"These are fake," Joe said.

"What about the picture?" Don asked.

"What picture?" Frank eyed Don suspiciously.

"I went to the police station to look for you guys. Con Riley was all upset about a missing school picture. He said he thought you might have taken it."

"I don't know what he's talking about," Frank said. He glanced at Joe.

Don snapped his fingers. "I just remembered. When I went to city hall to look for that file, I saw Chet and Callie going to the old bank building across the street. Then I saw Chet come out by himself."

"So?" Joe asked.

"So he looked like he'd been in a fight. He jumped into his car and drove away."

"*What?* You didn't try to stop him or find out where Callie was?" Don's attitude was making Frank angry.

"I thought it was strange, but I knew you wanted this file right away, and I forgot about the whole incident until just now."

Frank studied Don for a minute before saying, "We've got to find Chet."

Frank and Joe headed for the door.

"What's wrong?" Don asked.

"We don't believe Chet is Bobby Mock," Joe answered. "But we do believe he is in danger."

"And so is Callie," Frank said, closing and locking the door.

"I'll help look," Don said as he headed for his car.

"Check out the television station," Frank suggested. He was hoping to keep Don as far from the bank building as possible.

"Sure." Don hopped into his car and drove away.

Joe had barely fastened his seat belt when Frank threw the van into reverse and peeled out on the wet pavement. Slamming the shift into first, he made the van lurch forward.

"Slow down, or we'll hydroplane," Joe said. Joe was just as anxious to find Chet and Callie, but he didn't want them to wreck. Traveling fast on a wet road could cause the van's tires to rise up and slide on a pocket of water. Frank would lose control, and the brakes would be useless.

"Why did you send Don to the television station?" Joe asked.

"To get him out of the way."

"That doesn't answer my question."

"It'll have to do for now."

They reached the old Farmers and Merchants Bank building in a matter of minutes. The building stood twenty stories high and was one of the oldest in Bayport. The redbrick bank was undergoing a facelift, and scaffolding framed its structure like braces on teeth. A large sign in front of the building announced that by fall the old Farmers and Merchants Bank building would be the new Farmers and Merchants Downtown Mall.

Frank jumped from the van and ran into the building.

Frank didn't know what to believe about Don's story. Perhaps Callie had gotten into trouble, and Chet had gone for help. Some floors of the building had been ripped up to make way for a new elevator system and an atrium, and maybe Callie had fallen.

Why wouldn't Chet have run across the street to city hall or down the block to the police station for help?

Then, too, Don only remembered seeing Chet and Callie *after* Frank doubted that the adoption file was genuine. Don seemed to have a good memory when it suited him.

"Frank! Wait up!" Joe shouted.

Frank stopped.

"Here. We'll need these upstairs," Joe handed

Frank one of two police-issue flashlights—both were eighteen inches long. Not only would the flashlights provide good light, but they would also be heavy enough to use as clubs in case of trouble.

Frank flicked the flashlight on and started across the lobby, which was littered with power tools, buckets of paint and plaster, wood, and mottled tarps. The whole place smelled from the odor of paint and thinner. There was no one working that day because there was no electricity in the building. Only vital buildings had been reconnected.

"Why would Callie come here?" Joe asked as they made their way carefully through the maze of buckets and lumber.

"The assignment editor said she wanted to get a bird's-eye view of the damage. This building is tall, and it's in the right part of town."

They found the stairs, and minutes later they were standing on the roof, blinded by the glare of a bright yellow sun. The clouds had broken, and the sun was shining for the first time since the tornado had hit Bayport twenty-four hours earlier.

Frank walked to the edge of the roof to look down. On the street, twenty stories below, lay city hall, the police station, and many of the buildings that had been hardest hit by the tornado.

"No sign of Callie or Chet," Joe said, joining Frank. Then he pointed. "There's Don!"

Frank and Joe watched from nearly two hundred and twenty-five feet up as Don's small red sports car pulled in behind their black van. Don got out, glanced around, and stood still, apparently unsure of what to do. Finally he went into the bank building.

"I'll tell him we didn't find anything up here, and then we can start searching the other floors." Frank nodded, and Joe left the roof.

Frank stood scanning the area and wondering where Chet and Callie could be. Chet was his best friend, and Callie—well, Callie *was* his Number One Girl.

Then the thought that had been nagging at the back of his mind hit him full force. Frank ran for the roof door and then down the stairs, calling Joe's name.

Frank burst through the ground floor doors, the circular beam of his flashlight leaping before him. He dashed across the lobby, dodging the saw horses and buckets of paint.

"Frank! Over here!" Don shouted.

"What happened?" Frank asked as he joined Don and Joe.

Joe was just getting up, rubbing his chin.

"Mangieri—" Don began.

"That's the second time that nerd got the jump on me!" Joe said.

"Are you so sure it was Mangieri?" Frank asked Joe.

Joe stared at his brother, a puzzled expression on his face.

"Actually I didn't see anyone," Joe said. "I was coming around the corner and got blindsided. The first thing I knew, Don was standing over me. He said he saw Mangieri hit me."

"Why didn't you help Joe?" Frank angrily asked Don.

"I was clear across the lobby," Don replied defensively. "I saw what happened and ran to help, but Mangieri went down the hall. I thought I should help Joe first."

"What are you doing here anyway?" Frank's question was more of an accusation. "You were supposed to go to the TV station."

"I tried my phone. They must have got the system back on line sometime last night. I called the studio, and they told me Callie wasn't there. I thought I could help you two here."

"What's wrong?" Joe asked Frank.

"Nothing," Frank said quickly. "We've got to find Chet."

All three went outside.

"How can I help?" Don asked.

"Uh, you find Liz and see if she's seen Callie," Frank replied.

"Right," Don replied and hopped into his car. Frank headed for the van after Don had left.

"Are you going to tell me what's going on?" Joe asked as Frank pulled the van away from the building.

"How long have we known Don?" Frank asked.

"About three years, when he moved here from New York City."

"He's lived here for three years, and we don't know anything about him. Why is it that he's suddenly such an integral part of our lives?" Frank didn't wait for Joe to answer. "Why is it that Don conveniently shows up all the time? When you chased down Mangieri, when we were shot at, finding the so-called adoption file on Chet, and just now?"

Joe shrugged. He knew that Frank wasn't really seeking answers, only thinking out loud.

"How did he know about that kindergarten photo?"

"He said Officer Riley was yelling about it being missing," Joe replied.

"Pretty convenient, don't you think?"

"Quit playing around, Frank, and get to the point."

"The point is," Frank said slowly, "Don West is Bobby Mock!"

Chapter

8

JOE DIDN'T REPLY but sat silently thinking. He digested the information Frank had just given him and came to the same conclusion.

"That may explain the bruise on his cheek," Joe finally said.

"What?"

"When I fought with Bobby Mock in the ICU ward, I hit him with a good right to his left cheek. It would have left a pretty decent bruise."

"And when we were talking to Liz at the paper yesterday, Don knew that Bobby's mother had died when Bobby was three. How could he have known that?"

"Unless he *is* Bobby Mock," Joe conceded.

"What bothers me is how your shoulder got hurt," Frank said as they neared the Hardy home.

Joe rubbed his sore shoulder. "I know. I still can't explain it. It was like hitting a brick wall."

"Yesterday you said it felt like steel or something metal."

"Yesterday I wouldn't have believed a tornado could hit Bayport," Joe said. "Why are we going back home?"

"I want to check Dad's files again. I must have missed something this morning. Perhaps a newspaper photo or something on young Bobby Mock. We can't go to the police with what we know now. Chief Collig would laugh us out of his office."

Having arrived home, Frank immediately headed downstairs for his dad's files.

"Hey, I thought you were going to check Dad's files," Joe said at the top of the stairs.

Frank turned around and looked up at his brother. "I've already done a thorough search of his computer files. What I'm looking for can't be found on a disk. I'm checking his paper files one more time. Much easier to overlook a piece of paper."

"Oh," Joe said, heading for the kitchen. "Let me know if you need any help."

Frank smiled and shook his head. They had eaten breakfast approximately an hour earlier, but Joe was like a great white shark on a feeding frenzy that day.

Mr. Hardy's paper files were located in one corner of the basement the Hardys used for storage. He found the Mock file and sat down to read it. Although a fast reader, Frank forced himself to slowly reread the yellowing papers his father had typed years earlier. He searched for any clue as to the identity of Bobby Mock. He found nothing.

Frank sat back in the chair and sighed. Fenton Hardy was as meticulous about keeping accurate accounts of his cases as he was about solving them. There had to be something identifying Bobby Mock. A photo. A newsclipping. Anything.

"That's it!" Frank shouted as he snapped his fingers. Frank jumped up and ran up the stairs. His dad's old scrapbook. Actually, it was a scrapbook that the boys' aunt Gertrude kept on all the cases Mr. Hardy had solved throughout the years.

Once upstairs Frank hesitated outside his aunt's bedroom door. She would be very upset if she found out Frank had been snooping around in her bedroom. Frank shrugged and opened the door.

Aunt Gertrude's room was neat and tidy and smelled of talcum powder, hair spray, and expensive perfume. Frank flipped on the light switch and walked over to his aunt's desk. He opened the bottom drawer and pulled out a large red scrapbook. He sat at the desk and began flipping through the pages. He found newspaper articles and photos of the Leonard Mock case about a third of the way through the book.

Again Frank read the articles slowly, then he scrutinized the pictures carefully. Only four newspaper pictures existed: one showing Mock as he was being led into the police station shortly after he had killed Con Riley's partner, and three others as he was being led from the courthouse during his trial. Mock was surrounded by a large crowd of people each time.

Frank carefully removed the photos from the scrapbook and headed downstairs. He wanted to examine them in better light and with a magnifying glass. Perhaps he could recognize someone in the crowd. Perhaps he could even find Bobby Mock.

Frank reached the bottom of the staircase as a sudden pounding filled the house. He ran to the door and flung it open.

"Chet!" Frank shouted.

Chet stumbled forward. Frank caught him and led him inside to a chair in the living room.

Chet looked at Frank, his eyes glassy and red. "I—tried—to—find you—earlier." Chet grimaced as he tried to catch a deep breath.

"Where have you been?" Joe asked, joining them.

"Callie—she and I—Mangieri." Chet slumped back and passed out. A black object slid out from under his windbreaker and hit the floor.

"What's that?" Joe asked.

Frank picked up the object. "Callie's camcorder," he replied, holding up the video camera.

"Why would he have Callie's video camera?" Joe asked.

"More important, why doesn't Callie have her camcorder?" A sudden uneasiness came over Frank. He punched the Eject button and pulled the videocassette out. He walked over to the VCR, slid the tape in, and pressed Play. He grabbed the remote control and turned on the big-screen TV.

The first scenes of the videotape were from the day before and were of the damaged downtown area. Then the tape showed Frank, Joe, and Chet as they rescued the man from underneath the collapsed roof. Frank fast forwarded the tape until he recognized the outside of the abandoned Farmers and Merchants Bank building.

Callie and Chet had obviously gone to the top, and Callie had gotten her "bird's-eye view" of downtown Bayport. The scene flickered and then showed the lobby of the building looking out to the street.

"Hey!" the Hardys heard Chet shout on the video, and he suddenly ran across the picture.

Callie followed Chet with the camera.

Chet and a short man were grunting as they struggled and fought.

"Mangieri," Joe said.

Frank nodded.

"Chet!" Callie screamed.

The scene jumped again. This time the picture was turned sideways.

Callie must have dropped the camera, Frank thought, but it remained on.

Chet was overpowering the man, and Callie was helping when another figure entered the scene. Although the figure was silhouetted against the bank's picture window, Frank could tell that the second man was wearing a black raincoat and a ski mask.

Bobby Mock!

"You're dead, Morton!" Mock yelled.

Something about the voice sounded familiar to Frank, but he had to let the thought go for the moment—Mock brought a double fist down on Chet's back. Chet gasped and fell to the floor. Mangieri hit Chet twice, once across the left cheek and then a downward blow to the chin. A deep, sickening groan came from Chet as he tried to reach up and grab Mangieri. Chet missed and fell to the floor.

"Nooo!" Callie screamed.

Mock grabbed Callie in a throat lock.

"Callie!" Frank yelled and made a move for the television.

Joe pulled Frank back.

Frank was watching a recorded nightmare and was unable to do anything to help.

Callie screamed and struggled against Mock. Mock put his hand over Callie's mouth and yanked her head back. Callie reached back and tried hitting Mock in the eyes. Unsuccessful, she grabbed the ski mask and pulled it off.

Frank leaned closer to the big screen, hoping to

recognize the unmasked Bobby Mock. But the bright light from the outside created only silhouettes and shadows in the building.

Suddenly Callie gasped and stopped her struggling. Mock let loose, and Callie fell to the floor.

"Callie," Frank whispered, his mind whirling.

The scene jumped again. This time an unshaven, sweaty-looking Martin Mangieri stared into the camera, his face taking up the entire big screen.

"Want your girlfriend, Hardy? Come and get her before she becomes just another part of the big bang theory!" Mangieri laughed, his throaty cackle echoing throughout the house.

Then the big-screen television filled with static snow and hissed at the horrified Hardys.

Chapter

9

JOE TOOK THE REMOTE CONTROL from Frank and shut off the TV.

Frank sat staring at the blank screen, his eyes vacant.

Chet groaned.

The Hardys turned to see their friend sitting up in his chair.

"I'm sorry, Frank," Chet said, his voice weak.

"Did you get a look at the second man, at Bobby Mock?" Frank asked.

"No. Mangieri got in a couple of lucky shots, and all I saw were stars, Big Dipper and all." Chet rubbed his swollen jaw.

"I'll get some ice," Frank said.

"What happened? What took you so long to get here?" Joe asked.

"When I came to, Callie was gone, but her camcorder was still there. I played the tape back through the camera and saw what had happened. I had to find you, but I ran out of gas and walked the rest of the way."

Frank returned with a towel and ice. "Why didn't you go to the police?" he asked.

"Ow!" Chet groaned as he pressed the ice against his chin. "I knew Collig wouldn't let you look at the tape."

"Then you don't know what's going on?" Joe sat across from his old friend.

"What?" Chet's eyes darted between Frank and Joe.

Frank picked up the adoption file and handed it to Chet.

"Look at it."

Chet opened the file. "Hey! That's me," he said as he spotted the computerized image of himself. Then he read further.

A moment later he jumped up and flung the file at Frank.

"This is garbage!" he shouted.

"I agree," Frank replied. He reshuffled the file. "The copyright dates are all wrong."

"What?" Joe didn't like it when Frank kept clues from him.

"When we first looked at these," Frank began, holding up the file, "I noticed that the copyright date on the forms was from last year."

"So?" Chet asked, still pressing the ice against his chin.

"So, if your adoption had taken place years ago, the copyright on the forms would be from then or earlier." Frank let the file fall on the coffee table. "You've been set up."

Chet's eyes narrowed. Joe could tell his friend was thinking revenge. "Who did it?"

"Don West," Joe answered.

"We *think* it's Don West," Frank corrected.

Joe squinted at Frank in disbelief. He said in a low voice, "Who else? You were positive an hour ago."

Frank returned Joe's glare but remained silent.

"Don had access to the vital records department at city hall," Joe rattled off. "The pictures we found at Leonard Mock's apartment only go back three years—"

"About the same time Don West moved to Bayport," Chet finished.

Joe continued, "And this morning, when Don showed up here with the adoption file, he had a large bruise on his cheek on the same spot where I hit Bobby Mock last night." Joe paused. "So what's your problem, Frank?"

"It's too neat."

"You should talk about things being *too* neat, Mr. Clean."

"There's no such thing as the perfect crime *or* the perfect suspect," Frank replied calmly.

"Yeah, right. What's that from? Frank Hardy's Guide to Detective Work?" Joe spit out.

"I'm just saying we need to be cautious. First we have to find Callie."

"What did Mangieri mean about the big bang theory?" Chet asked.

"I don't know," Frank answered.

"Find Don West, and I bet we find Callie," Joe insisted.

"Maybe," Frank replied. "But if we go after West, and West isn't Mock, then we could be wasting time while Callie is—" Frank's voice broke off.

Joe and Chet exchanged a quick glance. There was no need for Frank to finish his sentence.

"One thing's for sure," Chet said. "We all know Mangieri's involved."

Frank's and Joe's heads jerked toward Chet.

"Leave it to Chet to point out the obvious," Joe said with a smile.

"Chet's right," Frank said. "We find Mangieri, and I bet we find Callie."

"And Bobby Mock," Joe added.

"Why is Mangieri even involved?" Chet asked.

"Money," Joe replied. "I'd still like to know how he got out of jail, what kind of deal he cut."

"That's a question Con Riley can answer," Frank answered.

"I say we find Mangieri and do a little knuckle

tap dance on his head.'' Chet stood to his full height. "I owe him a dance or two." He handed Frank the towel and ice and headed for the door. "Well?" he said as he stood with the door held open.

"Right with you, buddy," Joe said with a smile.

The trio jumped back into the black van. While Joe drove, Frank looked over the newspaper clippings. Besides being old and faded, they weren't very good photos. Frank pulled a small magnifying glass from the crime kit he kept under his portable laptop computer in the back of the van. He moved the glass slowly over the photos. After he had gone over each one carefully, he started over again.

"What are you looking for?" Chet asked over Frank's shoulder.

"A young kid."

"Why?"

"Mock was so attached to his son that it's possible he had him attend the trial. I'm trying to see if I can find a young kid in these news-clippings."

"Hey, you two going to help me look or what?"

They had reached the downtown area, and Joe was driving up and down streets where they shouldn't have been. The area was clearly posted as being off limits to keep looters away.

Chet joined Joe in the front while Frank stayed in the back.

"What's Frank doing back there?" Joe asked.

They were just about to turn onto Fifth Street when a siren pierced the air. Joe brought the van to a jarring halt as a police cruiser pulled up behind them.

A metallic voice boomed from the cruiser's speakers.

"All right. Step out of the van. With your hands in the open."

Frank, Joe, and Chet moved slowly from the van, their hands held open, palms out.

"Now stand against the van, legs spread. *And don't move.*"

"Officer—" Joe began.

He was jerked to one side and then slammed against the side of the van. He was ready to turn when he heard the click of a revolver and felt the cold steel of a barrel against his neck.

"Freeze!"

"All right, boys," began a second cop, "what are you doing here? This area is off limits."

"We were looking for a friend, Officer Stewart," Frank said, recognizing the slow drawl of the second policeman.

"Frank Hardy?" Officer Stewart turned Frank around. "Joe? Chet?"

"Yes," Frank said. "And we *are* looking for a friend."

"Tell your partner to ease up," Joe said.

"Cool it, Bud. I know these kids."

The first officer slowly let the hammer down on his .38, holstered it, and then walked back to the police cruiser.

Joe breathed for the first time in moments.

"Who you looking for?" Officer Stewart asked.

"Don West," Joe said quickly.

"We haven't seen him for a couple of hours, and we got worried," Frank added.

"The city manager's son?"

"Yes," Joe said.

"Haven't seen him," Officer Stewart said.

"Perhaps he made it home by now. We'll check there." Frank didn't want to hang around chatting with Officer Stewart while Callie was still in danger.

"I suggest all you boys head for home," Officer Stewart said. "The next cop who stops you may mistake you for looters, and you'll end up in jail."

"We'll be careful," Joe assured him.

"Hey, Stewart. Stop them. Chief Collig wants us to bring them in," Bud yelled from the cruiser, the mike of the police radio in his hand.

"Quick! In the van!" Frank shouted. He pushed Chet into the van, jumped in after him, and slammed the door shut.

Joe hopped into the driver's seat, threw the van into reverse, and peeled out. He made a hairpin turn in reverse, threw the van into first, and sped away.

"What's going on?" Chet demanded. He lost his balance in the turn and fell against the rear couch.

"Chief Collig threatened to put us into protective custody if he caught us working on this case," Frank explained.

"No one's behind us," Joe said as he checked the side-view mirror.

"We need a different set of wheels," Frank said. "You can bet Chief Collig will put out an all-points bulletin on this van."

"Aunt Gertrude's car," Joe suggested.

"No. I don't want to take a chance on the police being at our house looking for us."

"Hey! They won't be looking for my car," Chet said.

"Your car?" Joe didn't want to hurt his best friend's feelings, but Chet's car was little better than a junker. Joe had spent too many weekends under the hood of the sedan trying to keep it running. "But it's out of gas."

"No problem," Chet said. "We can siphon the gas from the van's reserve tank."

"Great idea," Joe said with a roll of his eyes.

Minutes later they pulled up behind Chet's car, which sat on a side road. At least, Joe thought, we won't be in traffic where a cop might see us.

Joe pulled a three-foot section of hose from the back of the van, unlocked the gas cap, shoved the hose down the tank, and took a deep breath. He didn't relish the thought of tasting gasoline.

"Here's the can." Frank placed a five-gallon gas can next to Joe.

"Thanks." But Joe didn't sound thankful. "Where's Chet?"

"He's rummaging around in his trunk for something," Frank replied.

"Yuck!" Joe spat gasoline as he put the hose into the gas can.

"Hey, Joe, I found it!" Chet dashed up to Joe.

"Found what?" Joe asked.

"The siphon hose." Chet held up a small hose that had a hand pump on one end—a pump that could manually create suction and drain the reserve tank.

"You mean I drank gasoline and you had a siphon pump all this time?" Joe's lips thinned, and his eyes narrowed.

"Well, sure. Dad bought this for me in case I needed gas from one of the other cars."

"Great," Joe mumbled.

The gas can filled, and Chet poured the gas into his car. He hopped in the front seat while Joe took off the air filter and primed the carburetor by pouring in a small amount of gasoline. He stepped back. After a couple of tries, Chet's car sputtered to life.

"Hop in, guys!"

Frank jumped in the back while Joe slid into the front.

"Where to?" Chet pulled the car away from the curb.

Frank sat silently. All the time Joe and Chet had been putting gas into the sedan, he was thinking about the videotape—Mangieri and Bobby Mock attacking Callie and Chet. Then Mangieri's face leering out at them, telling them that Callie would be a part of the big bang theory. Frank had always thought Mangieri was barely this side of crazy, but his last remark just didn't make sense.

"Frank!" Joe reached back and tapped Frank on the knee.

"Where to?" Chet repeated.

"What would Mangieri be doing with Bobby Mock?" Frank asked.

"Birds of a feather," Chet replied. "Creeps will hang around with creeps."

"You may be more right than you realize, Chet." Frank sat on the edge of the backseat. "Stop at the next convenience store."

"Why?" Joe asked.

"So we can do what we should have done in the first place," Frank replied. "Look up Mangieri's address in the phone book."

* * *

"Stop here," Frank said minutes later as Chet steered his sedan into a dead-end street in a run-down part of town.

"Why? I thought you said his house was in the middle of the block," Chet said as he slowed the car.

"I don't want them to see us pulling up," Frank replied.

Mangieri lived on the west side of Bayport in a low-rent area. All the houses on the dead end were semidetached. One wall was shared by two houses. Frank knew from the address that Mangieri's house would be in the middle of the block.

The trio got out of the car and silently shut their doors.

"Walk close to the other houses so they can't see us coming," Frank suggested.

Moments later they stood at the side of Mangieri's house.

"He's in the next half," Frank said. "Joe, you and Chet check the back in case they try to escape. I'll check the front door."

Frank moved silently and swiftly to Mangieri's front door. A screen door covered it. It was old, and the hinges were rusted. He knew he couldn't make a surprise entrance. He glanced in through the front window. Someone was sitting in a chair, his back to the door. In the dimness of the room, Frank couldn't tell if it was Mangieri or Mock.

"No back door," Chet announced as he walked up behind Frank.

Frank jumped back. His skin rippled with goose bumps. "Don't sneak up on me like that, Chet. And keep it down. Someone's inside." Then he noticed that Joe was missing. "Where's Joe?"

"He's checking out a back window. The glass was broken. He said he would enter through the back room and meet you inside."

"I wish he'd check with me first!" Frank had never liked Joe's impulsiveness. They should have worked out a plan of attack. Now he'd have to improvise and hope no one got hurt.

"I'm going to open this screen door real fast," Frank whispered to Chet. "You think you can kick the front door open?"

"No sweat." Chet stepped back and took a stance like a professional field goal kicker.

Frank would have laughed if the situation wasn't so serious. Instead, he only shook his head and peered back in through the window.

He saw Joe's head peek around the corner of an inner room. That was what Frank had been waiting for. He pulled open the screen door, and it creaked loudly.

"Now!" he barked to Chet.

Chet planted his foot next to the door knob, then kicked hard. The door groaned and snapped open, the knob and its lock falling to the ground.

Frank dashed in and confronted the figure sitting in the chair.

"Frank!" Joe shouted. "It's Callie."

Frank would have been relieved to find his girlfriend, but the digital timer on the bomb that was ticking at her feet showed that in thirty seconds they would all be dead.

Chapter

10

"DON'T TAKE ANOTHER STEP," Joe warned.

Joe pointed. Frank could see that the bomb was set to explode by any of three methods: the timer, a small, almost invisible trip wire, or if Callie moved.

Frank's eyes met Callie's, and he could see the terror that stared back at him.

He stepped over the trip wire.

"Don't move, Callie," he said calmly.

Twenty seconds.

"It's motion sensitive," Joe said.

"I saw it," Frank replied.

After dealing with terrorists, Frank knew enough about bombs to recognize the secondary fuse that hung in the center of a metal washer. If the fuse made contact, an electrical signal would surge through the mechanism, thus exploding the bomb.

Fifteen seconds.

"Okay, Callie," Frank began—he knew that talking to Callie would calm her—"I don't have time to untie you. I'm going to disconnect the primary wire going to the timer." Frank moved as he talked.

Ten seconds.

He tugged as gently as he could. The wire wouldn't budge.

"I think it's soldered together." Frank kept his voice calm.

Joe shoved his pocket knife between Frank and the bomb.

"No time." Frank had to keep his voice calm or Callie might panic.

Five seconds.

He clamped his fingers on the secondary fuse and lifted it through the metal washer—quickly but with a calm steadiness.

Three.

He tore the tape and the bomb from Callie's legs.

Two.

In one smooth motion he flung the bomb through the closed window in a perfect spiral, then covered Callie. The bomb shattered the glass as it flew outside.

Joe and Chet hit the floor.

First there was a bright burst of blinding white light, followed by a deafening explosion. Glass shards flew into the room, then dirt and dust.

A split second later the midafternoon day was calm once again.

"Callie!" Frank finished tearing the tape from around her legs. He gently pulled the tape from her mouth.

"Oh, Frank!" she cried.

Frank ripped off the tape that bound her wrists. Callie jumped up and threw her arms around his neck.

"Frank! I thought I was dead!" She continued to hug Frank.

"You're okay, Callie. You're okay." Frank put his arms around her. "Nothing's ever going to happen to my Number One Girl."

Before Frank had time to react, Callie kissed him hard.

"Enough already," Joe grumbled. "Let's get out of here before the cops arrive."

Frank attempted to move, but Callie hung on.

"Don't let go," she said, terror in her voice.

"We've got to go," Frank said gently. "I'll explain later."

Chet was already in the car, its engine revving. Several people from the neighborhood were gathering around, looking first at the small crater in the front yard, then at the blown-out window, and last at the four teenagers peeling away in the sedan.

Chet and Joe were in front. Callie sat close to Frank in back, her hand holding his in a firm grip.

"The police have orders to take us in," Frank explained.

"Arrest you?" Callie was still shaken, and there was a tremor in her voice.

"Not arrest us. Chief Collig doesn't want us on this case." Frank put his arm around Callie's shoulders. "Someone is out to kill Dad—and our friends."

"Wh-why?"

"To settle an old score. A blood law."

"A what?" Chet asked from the front seat.

Joe spoke up. "In Anglo-Saxon days they didn't have police or courts or jails. They relied on what they called 'blood law.' It's also known as 'an eye for eye.' Retribution."

"But wh-who—wh-what—" Callie held back a sob.

Frank quickly explained about Leonard and Bobby Mock, then about the videotape.

"Do you remember anything after Mock and Mangieri kidnapped you?"

Callie took a breath. She had to control her breathing while she spoke. "I—just remember seeing Chet fighting with Mangieri." She sobbed. "Then I tried to help. Someone grabbed me from behind—"

"Bobby Mock," Joe added.

"I guess."

"Did you get a good look at his face? Was it Don West?" Frank asked.

"*Don West?* I—I don't know. I was choking. I couldn't really see. I don't even remember tearing the mask off." Callie gasped. "You don't really think that Don is Bobby Mock."

"The evidence is pointing that way."

"Poor Liz," Callie said.

"What happened at Mangieri's?" Frank asked.

"When I came to, I was in that chair. Mangieri was standing in front of me with that bomb. He said Bobby had made it. Then he set the timer and left."

"What did he set the timer for?" Frank asked.

"Five minutes. Why?"

"That tells us how much of a head start he had," Joe answered.

"Why would he be foolish enough to kill Callie in his own apartment?" Chet asked.

"That's what's bothering me," Frank replied.

"Why not? It makes sense to me," Joe said with a knowing air.

"Explain it." Frank was skeptical.

"It makes sense if Mangieri is really Bobby Mock."

Frank was even more skeptical. "Why Mangieri and not Don West?"

"Mangieri has disliked us from the day he moved into Bayport over four years ago. Besides, before he got kicked out of school, he was a photographer for the yearbook," Joe answered.

"That's right," Chet blurted out. "I remember him taking pictures of us at the beach for some project he was working on."

"That project was us," Joe added.

"That sounds fine," Frank said with reservation. "However, who's the guy in the raincoat and ski mask who tried to shoot us and then helped kidnap Callie?"

Joe slumped in his seat. Hard as he had tried before, Joe rarely matched Frank's logic for looking at a problem from different angles. Joe liked to move straight through a problem. Frank liked to go over, under, or around a problem.

"What we need to do is find Mangieri and Don and get this thing settled before someone gets killed," Frank said.

"Like our father."

"Stop at that convenience store," Frank ordered Chet.

"Why?"

"I'll tell you in about five minutes."

Frank had the others wait in Chet's car. He shoved a quarter into the pay phone outside the convenience store and punched a familiar number.

"Hello," Con Riley said at the other end of the phone."

"Con," Frank said, then paused. He was glad that Officer Riley was at home.

"What is it, Frank?"

"I need a big favor."

Static hissed back at Frank. He knew that Con was thinking, considering what Chief Collig might say, what might happen to his career.

"First tell me what it is."

"Callie was almost killed a short while ago. A bomb at Mangieri's place."

"Why didn't you call that in, Frank?"

Con's tone was as authoritative as it was agitated. Like an adult's.

"I should have, Con." Frank tried to sound genuinely sorry. "But I was afraid Chief Collig would put Joe and me in jail."

"Do you blame him?"

"No."

"I'm listening. But don't be too sure I won't hunt you down and throw you in jail myself."

"Fair enough." Frank took a breath. He had to present this just right to Con or the police veteran would be true to his word. Then Frank and Joe would be helpless to stop Mock from killing their father.

"Dad and Mom and Aunt Gertrude were supposed to have left Philadelphia earlier today, but they haven't arrived."

"You think Mock has Fenton?" Con sounded concerned.

Frank was relieved at the change of tone in Con's voice.

"I don't know, but Mock isn't an amateur. That

bomb was professional, Con. What I need, what Joe and I need, is for someone with official jurisdiction to contact the highway patrol to see where Dad's car is.''

"Then what, Frank?"

"I need to get into city hall tonight."

"And?"

"And I need access to the police computer."

"I don't have a problem with your first request, Frank, but let me see if I understand you about the other two. You want me to help you break into city hall in the middle of night and then sneak you into police headquarters to use our main computer?"

Frank didn't hesitate. "Yes."

"It would be easier to deliver the moon, Frank."

"I know, Con. But we're talking about my father's life. We're talking about one of your closest friends."

Again the line hissed static at Frank. The moments seemed like long minutes.

"Okay." Con sighed. "This is for Fenton. And for Stan Williams."

"Who?"

"My partner who was killed."

"I understand," Frank replied.

Frank then explained to Con that he intended to get into city hall through one of the basement windows in the rear of the old building and then make his way to the old file room in the basement.

He wanted to find the original adoption file for
Bobby Mock.

He returned to the sedan and quickly explained
his plan to the other three. They decided to meet
back at the Hardy home at nine P.M., after dark.
Then they took Callie home. Chet dropped Frank
and Joe off at their van, and then he went home,
also.

"Look who we have here," Joe said as he
spotted Don West's red sports car sitting in their
driveway. "He's been pretty smart up until now."

"We've still got to prove he really is Bobby
Mock," Frank warned Joe.

"No problem." Joe stopped the van and hopped
out. He checked Don's car.

"Where is he?" Joe asked as he followed Frank
to the house.

"Right here," Don said as he stepped from
behind a hedge, holding a hunting rifle aimed
straight at Joe!

Chapter
11

"TAKE IT EASY, DON," Frank said, holding up his hands. "We don't want to hurt you."

"Hurt me?" Don laughed, but Frank could tell that it wasn't the type of laugh that results from something being funny. Don's laugh arose from nervousness and fear. "That's just like you Hardys. I have a thirty-thirty deer rifle aimed at Joe's heart, and you threaten me."

"We know who you are," Joe said bluntly.

"Yeah? Well, why don't you tell me who you think I am!" Don shouted.

Frank could see the tension in Don's eyes and the beads of sweat that had formed on his forehead. The finger squeezing the trigger of the deer rifle unfolded and then folded around the trigger again. Frank didn't know Don very well, but he knew enough about human nature to sense that Don was a fuse about to blow.

"You're Bobby Mock," Joe announced.

"I've been told that's what you believe," Don replied, his voice nearly cracking.

"Who told you?" Frank asked, suddenly aware that someone had betrayed them.

"Liz. She got a message from Callie and then called me."

Frank took a step to Don's left. "I don't believe you. Just like I don't believe the story about the box hitting you in the cheek. You got that bruise when Joe hit you at the hospital last night."

Watching Frank's move, Joe stepped to Don's right. They had to distract Don so one of them could jump him and take the gun away.

"Stay where you are, Joe!" Don ordered through clenched teeth. "You too, Frank. I'll use this if I have to." Don raised the barrel of the gun for emphasis.

"You going to kill us in cold blood in front of our house?" Joe asked.

"No," Don answered calmly. "I'm not going to kill you."

"We're not going to let you kill our father, either," Joe said.

"I don't want to kill your father," Don said.

"What?" Joe blurted out, confused. "But—"

"I don't want to kill anybody. I'm not Bobby Mock."

Frank saw the tension drain from Don, and the finger folded around the trigger of the rifle relaxed. Don lowered the rifle and held it down in front of him.

"I'm sorry," he said. "I didn't know what else to do." He handed the rifle to Joe.

Stunned, Joe stared at Don for a second, then slowly took the rifle from Don's hands. He looked at Frank, who only returned his questioning gaze.

"I've admired the two of you ever since I moved to Bayport. You've got a pretty mean reputation for bringing in the bad guys. When I heard you were after me, I was afraid I wouldn't be able to explain." Don paused and sighed.

"Explain what?" Frank asked.

"That I'm not Bobby Mock. That I didn't plant the bogus file on Chet. I really found it at city hall, and a box really did fall and hit me."

"How did you know when Bobby Mock's mother died?" Joe asked, gripping the rifle in his hands.

"I did the research for Liz before she called you two. It was in an old article about Leonard Mock's trial."

"He's right," Frank said with a nod of his head. "I read the same article this morning in Dad's file."

"That still doesn't explain why you've taken such an interest in us the past two days," Joe said, still skeptical.

"I told you—I admire you guys. Because of my

dad's occupation, I've had to move around a lot, and I never really made friends very easily, never joined any clubs or went out for sports. I was real lucky to find Liz. When I saw that I might be able to help you two, I leapt at the chance." Don smiled. "I guess I should have looked before I leapt, huh?"

Frank laughed. "I believe you," he said. He looked at his brother. "Joe?"

Joe stared at Don and then glanced over at Frank. He fingered the safety switch on the rifle and was surprised to find that it was locked. He looked at Don and smiled. "Yeah, I guess I believe you, too. But that leaves one question. Who told Liz we thought you were Bobby Mock?"

"I guess the *real* Bobby Mock set that one up," Don said, taking a deep breath. He held out his hand to Joe. "I'm sorry I pointed that rifle at you."

Joe grabbed Don's hand in a firm grip. "I understand. You still want to help us find Bobby Mock?"

"You mean it?" Don asked excitedly.

"How do you feel about back alleys and breaking into city hall?" Joe said as they headed into the house.

"What?" Don replied, a puzzled expression on his face.

The alley behind city hall was littered with garbage thrown about by the previous day's tornado.

Frank, Joe, Callie, Chet, and Don zigzagged their way through the mess to the rear of the building.

Don and Joe had gone in Don's sports car while Frank, Callie, and Chet had used Chet's sedan. They parked the cars several blocks away and made their way moving from shadow to shadow in the moonless night.

Joe had wanted Don to "borrow" his father's keys to city hall, but Frank had vetoed the idea on the grounds that, if caught, Mr. West could be implicated. Joe still liked his idea, especially after stubbing his toe several times on the garbage.

"Here," Frank said, and he put his arms out to halt the group.

"How can you see?" Chet said, frustrated.

"He's got the eyes of a cat," Joe answered.

Frank ignored both of them. He knelt down by the basement window and pushed against the glass. He didn't really expect it to be unlocked, but he was hoping it might have been broken by the storm.

He wrapped his hand in his handkerchief, broke the glass, and then unlocked the window.

He checked up and down the alley. He just hoped that Con was standing out in front of the police station to distract any other cops who might patrol the alley.

He slid in across the window and jumped to the floor. Callie followed, then Joe and Don. Chet was a tighter fit, but he did make it through.

Frank shut the window.

"Now you can turn your penlight on," Frank said to Joe. "But keep the beam on the floor."

"I've done this before," Joe reminded him pointedly.

"The old records section is in the subbasement," Don said. "I can show you where I found the bogus file on Chet."

Once downstairs, Joe tried a light switch. To their surprise, the overhead fluorescent lights flickered on.

"This might be easier than we thought," Joe said.

"Okay," Frank said as the others formed a semicircle in front of him. "Don, how did you find the file on Chet."

"Everything's on computer. I just waited until the computers came back on-line and then searched for the case file number."

"How did you do that?" Frank asked.

"I pulled up the file on Robert Edward Mock," Don explained.

"You didn't find the right file," Frank announced.

"How do you know?" Don asked.

Frank pulled the folded newspaper clippings from his shirt pocket. "Because of these," he announced. "Look." He laid the news photos on a desk. "In all four news photos, Mock is surrounded by a crowd of people."

"That makes sense," Callie said. "Mock's trial was the biggest sensation to hit Bayport in years."

Frank smiled at Callie. He returned his gaze to the photos. "I missed it the first few times I went over them, but then I spotted him."

"Who?" Chet asked.

"Bobby Mock. There." Frank pointed at a kid in the first photo who was half hidden by the crowd pressing around Leonard Mock. "And there." He pointed at the second photo, and again, the same kid was present. "And there, and there." In the third and fourth photos, the kid was more visible.

For the first time they all got a good look at a young Bobby Mock, his white blond hair uncombed, a halfmoon birthmark just above his upper lip.

"He's tall for six years old," Joe said.

"That's been our mistake from the beginning," Frank said. "We all assumed Bobby Mock was our age. He's not five in those photos. He's at least eleven or twelve."

"That means we're looking for someone who's twenty-three or twenty-four," Joe announced.

"I still don't understand how I picked up the wrong file," Don said.

"It's not your fault. You got the file you were meant to find," Frank replied. "Didn't they used to write all the case numbers in a big log?" Frank asked Don.

"They still do," Don answered. Then he snapped his fingers. "Bobby Mock's real case file could be found in the old handwritten log."

"Right," Frank replied with a smile.

Don darted down a row of shelves and disappeared. He returned moments later.

"Here it is," he announced, holding up a thick two- by three-foot book. "The old case log." He laid the book gently on the desk as though it were a valuable volume of literature.

Frank flipped through the yellowing pages. "Look at this." The others looked over Frank's shoulders. "Mock, Robert Edward, adoption granted."

"Does it say who adopted Mock?" Callie asked.

"No." Frank leaned up. "But it gives us the case number."

"Chet, I'll need your help getting the file box down from the shelf," Don said as he wrote down the case number. Then he and Chet disappeared toward the rear of the file room.

"That still doesn't explain why Mangieri's involved," Callie said.

"For money," Frank replied. "What bothers me is how he got out of jail," Frank added.

"Got it!" Don announced as he and Chet trotted back up to the desk. He handed the file to Frank, who placed it on the desk. He turned the cover back.

Staring back at them was a small photo of the same kid they had seen in the news photos, his eyes dark with fear and worry, his face a scowl, his hair mussed.

"Bobby Mock," Frank said.

"He looks so scared—and lonely," Callie whispered.

Frank flipped over the first page. The second page was a court order taking custody of Bobby away from Leonard Mock.

The third page was a request by a young couple to adopt Bobby Mock and legally change his name.

The fourth page granted the request.

Frank cleared his throat and said, "Robert Edward Mock then became—"

"Robert Edward Stewart," a deep voice said from behind them.

They all spun around. Officer Stewart stood at the base of the stairs, his .357 drawn and pointing at the group.

"Now, who'll be the first to die?" Stewart asked with a smile.

The fluorescent light bounced off Stewart's white blond hair and created a shimmering halo over his head like that of an angel of death.

Chapter

12

"I ALWAYS LIKED the meticulous way you thought, Frank," Stewart said. A sly grin spread across his face. "I made only one mistake—keeping that old file down here."

"That wasn't your only mistake," Frank said. "Officer Riley knows we're down here, and he'll—"

"Ah, yes. Officer Riley," Stewart interrupted. "My *partner*. Supposed to be watching the front, isn't he? He told me what you were up to, thought I would want to help, being a fellow cop and all. Quite a weird twist of fate, huh? I mean the son of the man who killed his partner now kills him."

"*What?*" Joe blurted.

"Don't get so excited, Joe," Stewart said. "He's not dead—yet. Let's just say he's resting. He's at the top of the stairs, unconscious. He's safe. For now."

"How did you get the file changed?" Frank asked.

"My first job was working the night shift at city hall," Stewart answered without hesitation. "That's when we hit on the plan."

"Plan?" Callie asked.

"The plan to set Chet up to throw us off," Frank answered. Frank shifted and Stewart braced himself. "You're nervous, Officer Stewart."

"I'd be foolish not to be nervous."

"What now?" Callie asked.

"I say we rush him," Don growled.

"Yeah? You plan to be the first hero to die? I left a message with Liz that you were me." Stewart let out a bone-chilling laugh and waved the magnum among the five teenagers.

"How did you get Officer Riley in here?" Joe asked.

Stewart shrugged. "I suggested we check up on you kids, make sure you were okay. We told the cop on the night shift to take a break, that we would watch the place for a while."

"You're not getting away with this," Frank said.

"I've already gotten away with this," Stewart replied, smiling. "Riley doesn't know what hit him." Stewart held up his gun, and Frank could see a little blood on the butt end. "However, that's not the story Chief Collig will hear. No, what really happened is that Officer Riley and his partner, that's me, thought we heard looters breaking into city hall. When we investigated, gunfire erupted, and Officer Riley was killed, but not before he killed three of the looters." Stewart pulled a second gun from behind him. "This is Officer Riley's gun. I, of course, killed Frank and Joe Hardy."

"What about our guns?" Joe asked with a smirk.

Stewart put Officer Riley's gun down on the desk. He knelt down, keeping his dark eyes and the silver magnum trained on the group, and pulled a snub-nosed .38 from an ankle holster. "Here, catch!"

Stewart threw the gun at Joe, and Joe caught the gun and pointed it at the police officer.

"Don't insult my intelligence, Joe. It's empty. And now it has your fingerprints on it. Hand it back to me. Gently."

Joe looked at the pistol. He began to hand the gun to Stewart, then he threw it down one of the aisles, where it clanked to the concrete floor and slid under one of the shelves of files.

"That wasn't very smart, Joe." Stewart's triumphant grin twisted into an angry frown.

"You'll never find it under all those files," Joe said calmly. "How are you going to explain that one, wise guy?"

Stewart straightened himself and grabbed Riley's gun.

"Let's see, which of you gets killed by Officer Riley, and which of you is the lucky one that is killed by the hero, Officer Stewart?"

"You're not going to kill us?" Don said, a little cry in his voice.

Joe turned to Don. He was surprised to see Don cowering, backing up, frightened. He began to regret having Don along.

"Pl-please," Don stammered. "D-d-don't kill me. *Please*."

"You coward." Joe sneered.

"I don't want to die!" Don blurted out and fell to his knees.

Joe was disgusted.

"Stand up, West," Stewart ordered.

"No, no, no," Don cried. Then he turned to Joe. "Don't let him kill me."

Joe was tempted to hit Don, to shut him up. Then he saw the slightest wink from Don's eye. Suddenly Joe knew that Don was only pretending to distract Stewart.

"I said stand up!" Stewart moved toward Don.

Don grabbed for Stewart's knees, and Joe kicked out at the magnum in Stewart's right hand. Stewart stepped back, and Don landed on the floor. Joe's kick connected with the magnum, and the gun flew from Stewart's hand and exploded.

"*No!*" Callie screamed and fell to the floor.

"Callie!" Frank rushed to Callie. The bullet had grazed her left temple.

"Don't move, punks," Stewart growled. He pulled back the hammer of Riley's gun and held it to Don's head.

Joe stopped and stepped back, his hands held up. "Okay, just take it easy."

"I'll take it easy, punk," Stewart spit out. He knelt and picked up his magnum. "Enough of this! Time to die."

"Stewart!" Officer Riley gasped from the top of the stairs.

He stumbled down, nearly falling. Frank saw a thin line of dried dark blood on the side of his forehead.

"Drop it, Stewart," Riley said with authority.

Stewart laughed and fired Riley's gun at Riley. Con flew backward and slid down the stairs.

"No!" Frank yelled and leapt for Stewart. Stewart swung around and caught Frank across the temple. Frank slumped to the floor.

"Frank!" Callie screamed and crawled over to him, cradling the unconscious Frank in her arms.

"Change of plans, folks." Stewart cackled. "Officer Riley was killed with his own gun by Frank Hardy." He pointed the .357 automatic magnum at Frank. "And I killed Frank Hardy!"

Chapter

13

CON RILEY KICKED out just as Stewart started to pull the trigger. The bullet hit the ceiling and bits of concrete and gray dust fell on Frank and Callie. Riley groaned and collapsed.

Joe sprang on Stewart and knocked him against a desk. He clamped his hands on both of the man's wrists to keep Stewart from pointing the .357 at him.

Don ran to Frank. "You okay?" he asked.

"Yeah," Frank groaned. Then he turned and saw that Joe was now struggling with Stewart. "Joe—"

Don ran to help Joe. The magnum exploded again, and Don yelled as he grabbed for his shoulder.

Joe turned. He was distracted just long enough

to give Stewart time to twist around. Joe's back was now against the desk.

Joe pushed Stewart away, and he flew backward, tripping over Riley and falling onto the stairs. He dropped Riley's gun. Joe kicked it away.

Stewart raised the magnum and fired. Joe dived behind the desk, the corner exploding in wooden splinters and chips.

Joe popped back up immediately, but Stewart was gone. Joe could hear the fleeing footsteps of the bad cop as he reached the top of the stairs.

Joe ran to Don. "You okay?"

"Yeah, it grazed my shoulder. It just burns a little." Don grimaced. "I'll be okay. Check Riley."

Joe dashed to Officer Riley. He checked the police veteran's chest and was shocked to find no blood. Joe ripped open Con's shirt to find a bulletproof vest.

"Is he okay?" Frank asked, joining Joe.

"Yes. How's Callie?"

"I'm fine," Callie said, holding Frank's handkerchief to her head.

"Look at this, Frank." Joe directed Frank's attention to the bulletproof vest.

"So?"

"So I thought I hit something hard, like metal, when I fought with Bobby Mock at the hotel room. Remember?"

"It wasn't metal," Frank said. "It was a bulletproof vest."

"Right."

"Is there a phone down here, Don?" Frank asked.

"Yeah," Don said.

"Good. Call the police station. Tell them we have an officer down and need assistance."

Frank and Joe walked into the darkened entryway of their home. Joe flipped on the living room light and threw himself in an overstuffed chair.

"I feel like I've been awake forever," Joe said, sighing.

"Me, too," Frank agreed as he yawned.

"You make sure the doors and windows are locked," Chief Collig ordered Officer Murphy. Murphy disappeared down the hallway as the police chief stood in front of Frank and Joe.

"What now?" Frank asked.

"Now you two go to bed and let real cops handle police business. You're lucky I don't throw you in jail for obstruction of justice." Frank didn't like the slight smile on the chief's face.

"What about Officer Riley?" Joe asked.

"He may be guarding a crosswalk for a while—"

"Is he all right?" Frank interrupted.

"The bulletproof vest saved his life. He's got a couple of cracked ribs, but he'll survive."

"Good." Frank sighed.

"Doors and windows locked," Officer Murphy reported as he entered the living room.

"Outside," Chief Collig said, pointing behind himself. He turned to Frank and Joe. "You two get a good night's sleep," Chief Collig said, his voice soft.

"What about Stewart?" Frank asked.

"We'll find him. Officer Murphy will be outside in his patrol car. You two *stay* home. Good night." Then he walked out the door.

"Now what?" Joe asked.

"Stewart's not going to try anything," Frank said, standing.

"How do you know?"

"He wants us too badly to risk getting caught at our house."

"You have a plan?"

"We'll take Chief Collig's advice and then sneak out in the morning," Frank said as he headed up the stairs.

Joe followed. He didn't know what Frank had planned, if anything, but he was too tired to care.

Frank and Joe rose at six A.M. Frank looked out his bedroom window. A patrol car sat at the curb. Frank smiled. Officer Murphy's head was back against the headrest, his eyes closed, his mouth open.

"He's asleep," Frank said.

"How do you plan to get the van out without waking him?" Joe asked.

"Put it in neutral and let it roll out into the

street, then start the engine and peel out. By the time Officer Murphy realizes what's happening, we'll be gone with the wind.''

"Solid," Joe replied.

They headed down the stairs.

"I want to call Callie and make sure she's okay," Frank said.

Frank picked up the receiver and punched in Callie's private number. Then he noticed the flashing red light on the answering machine. Someone had called. Frank put the receiver down and punched the Play button on the answering machine.

A moment later Laura Hardy's voice spoke from the machine, "Frank. Joe. We got your message, and your father wanted me to call to tell you he's renting a car and driving back after he sleeps a couple of hours. It's"—she paused—"eleven o'clock now. Your father said he should be in around seven or seven-thirty in the morning. He'll meet you at that truck stop. He said you'd know which one. Aunt Gertrude and I are driving back tomorrow. You two take care. 'Bye.''

Frank shut off the machine.

"What message?" Joe asked.

"We didn't leave a message," Frank said sternly.

"Stewart," Joe hissed.

"Right. Mom must have called before we got home last night. I knew I should have checked the answering machine." Frank picked up the phone and punched the number of the Philadelphia hotel where his parents were staying.

"What are you doing?" Joe asked.

"Calling Mom. Perhaps she knows what the message said."

"How are you going to ask her about that without alarming her about Stewart?"

"I'll think of something."

Mrs. Hardy and Aunt Gertrude had already checked out of the hotel, a desk clerk informed Frank.

"What now?" Joe asked.

"First we get past Officer Murphy," Frank replied and headed for the kitchen.

"We've got to find Stewart and fast," Joe said.

"If Stewart's the one who left that message for Dad, then he'll be waiting at the truck stop."

"Which one?" Joe asked as they stopped at the back door.

"We'll try the one on Highway Nine; that's where Dad would come in from Philadelphia."

They ran out the back door and sneaked around to the front. Using the van as cover, they opened the side door and hopped into the vehicle.

Joe put the van in neutral and silently rolled it out into the street. Then he flipped the ignition switch forward, fired the van to life, threw the shift into first, and stomped on the accelerator. The tires screamed as the van lurched forward and sped off.

Frank didn't know how Officer Murphy had reacted, and he didn't care. He could imagine Chief Collig's volcanic reaction when Murphy reported the incident, though.

Five minutes later Joe guided the van into the large parking lot of Trucker's Pit Stop, a truck stop just west of Bayport.

"Look for a rental car, something with Pennsylvania tags," Frank said.

Joe slowly snaked the van down and through the rows, but they found nothing.

"Maybe he's not here yet," Joe said after several frustrating passes.

"He should have been, if this is the truck stop Mom was referring to. Try around the back."

Joe turned and headed to the rear, back behind the large garage and oversize car washes.

"Look!" Joe said, pointing to a light blue sedan.

Martin Mangieri, his telltale black leather jacket and long dirty blond hair, was shutting the trunk of the sedan.

Joe pressed the accelerator, and the van lurched, moved, the tires squealing. Mangieri turned and horror filled his eyes as the black van sped toward him.

He ran to the front of the sedan and hopped into the driver's seat.

Joe hit the brakes, and Frank jumped from the van. He grabbed the door handle on the driver's side of the sedan and lifted it just as Mangieri locked the door. Then Joe saw his father's brief-case lying on the seat next to Mangieri.

"He's got Dad!" Frank yelled.

Mangieri smiled as he started up the car. He threw the car into reverse and shouted through the rolled-up window, "Your old man's dead, Hardy! *Dead!*"

Chapter

14

FRANK SLUGGED the driver's window but managed only to hurt his knuckles.

Mangieri laughed, and the blue sedan jetted away from the curb.

Frank hopped back into the van, and Joe turned it around.

"Dad's briefcase is in the front seat. I think Mangieri's got Dad in the trunk."

The Hardys always kept the engine and transmission finely tuned, and the hot-rodded van responded with a clean, even burst of speed and power. The van swooped down behind the blue sedan like a black bird of prey.

Mangieri glanced into the rearview mirror. Joe could see the fear in his eyes. Mangieri must have given the car more gas because it, too, suddenly burst forward. In a second he was putting some distance between it and the van.

"He's not going to slow down!" Frank yelled above the roar of the van's fireball engine.

"That sedan's faster than it looks."

The sedan jerked to the left, then back to the right.

Joe saw why a split second later. A large branch torn from a tree sat in the middle of the road. Joe didn't have time to turn the van. They slammed into the branch and flew into the air.

"Whoa!" Frank yelled and clutched his seat. The van smacked back down on the pavement, the shocks groaning and creaking against the sudden impact. Then the van began to swerve.

Joe fought to keep the van under control. He let up on the gas pedal and lightly pressed the brakes. The large vehicle responded to Joe's gentle touch and straightened out.

Mangieri had used the extra time to gain more distance. Joe again pressed the accelerator hard. The gap between the two vehicles slowly and steadily decreased.

Frank grabbed the CB and turned the channel button to nine, the emergency channel.

"I'm calling the cavalry," Frank announced as he pressed the button on the hand mike. "Mayday! Mayday! Any Bayport police. This is Frank Hardy. We are chasing a suspected kidnapper in a stolen car." Frank glanced at the corner street sign as the van zoomed past it. It was just a blur, but he was able to make out the letters well enough to say, "We're on Highway Nine headed west. The suspect's car is a light blue, late model sedan. Pennsylvania plates. A rental. I repeat, we are chasing a stolen car. The kidnap victim is inside, he may be hurt. Need assistance." He released the button. Frank was set to repeat the announcement when the CB buzzed.

"This is Bayport Police Department, please repeat your message. Over."

Frank began to repeat his message but was cut short.

"Frank Hardy!" boomed the angry voice of Chief Collig. "Where are—"

Frank shut off the CB.

"So much for that idea."

"Where's he headed?" Joe asked above the noise.

"Looks like away from Bayport," Frank replied.

Joe glanced at the speedometer. The digital speedometer flashed 70 MPH.

"C'mon, baby," Joe said under his breath to the van. He pressed the accelerator closer to the floor.

They inched closer to the sedan. The light blue digital speedometer flashed 75, then 80. Every nerve and muscle in Joe's body seemed to contract at once. One bad move—a quick swerve by Mangieri, another branch in the road, anything to cause Joe to lose control—and the black van would become their coffin.

When the van was a foot from the blue sedan's rear bumper, Mangieri's car responded with more speed.

Joe's eyes flashed. He couldn't safely go any faster.

Mangieri slowed a little. Joe pulled the van to the left and tried to edge up to Mangieri. He had to back off when he saw oncoming traffic headed toward him on the two-lane highway.

"Try to get on the other side of him!" Frank shouted.

Joe had been thinking the same thing. With traffic on his left and the van on the right, Mangieri would be trapped. Joe whipped the van to the right and was soon beside Mangieri.

"He's trapped!" Frank said.

Mangieri jerked his head from left to right.

Joe glanced at the car. He could see his father's leather briefcase lying on the passenger seat.

Just then Mangieri stomped the brake, sending the rear of the car into a violent fishtail. The sedan bounced off the van, and hot, white sparks shot out. The cars whipped back and made contact again. This time a high-pitched scream accompanied the crash as the sedan's fender was torn from its body.

Joe pushed his brake flat, and the van jerked, slowing.

Mangieri tried to speed up, but his car had lost its power.

"Now it's our turn," Joe announced.

"Careful," Frank warned. "Dad could be in the trunk."

"I'm just going to get in front of him," Joe said.

He pressed down on the accelerator and easily began to pull ahead of the sedan. He glanced over at Mangieri.

"Look out!" Frank yelled.

Joe jerked his eyes forward. The shoulder of the road had turned into an exit ramp, which curved sharply to the right. Joe's mind raced with decisions. Mangieri was on his left, the exit was on his right, and fifty feet straight ahead was a concrete pillar. He had to get in front of Mangieri before he hit the pillar or else he'd have to go off at the exit ramp.

Joe knew they didn't have enough time to give the van more speed to get all the way in front of Mangieri. They'd have to take the exit. He lightly pressed the brakes and felt the brake pads grab the wheel disks. They had to slow before taking the sharp right turn.

Just then Joe's foot and the brake pedal slammed to the floor as the brakes turned to mush.

"The brakes are gone!" Joe yelled. "I can't turn into the exit. We'll flip over."

Dead ahead the concrete pillar rose like a giant tombstone.

Chapter

15

JOE PRESSED ON the emergency brake pedal. He did it slowly or else the brakes would grip the wheels in a deadly lock that would send the van rolling like a large tin can.

The van jerked and then slowed. At the last possible second Joe spun the wheel and made the edge of the ramp. Mangieri had disappeared over the hill. The van coasted to a stop.

Frank brought his fist down on the dash. "What happened to the brakes?" His question was almost an accusation.

"I don't know!" Joe shouted back.

He hopped from the van and dived under the front end. He rose a moment later, a small, oil-drenched twig in his hands.

"What is it?" Frank asked.

"This must have broken off the branch we hit and stuck in the brake line," he explained, showing Frank the twig.

"Brake lines are metal," Frank replied.

"Not the brake lines going directly into the brake cylinder of the wheel. They're rubber."

"Can you patch it?"

"No." Joe got in and slammed the door shut. He snapped the twig with his fingers and tossed the broken pieces out the window. "We'll have to get a new one. But not right now." Joe turned the van in a hard right turn and hit the accelerator to go back onto the highway.

Frank knew that Joe was an expert enough driver to continue the chase using the emergency brake.

"Where is he?" Joe asked as they topped a Hill. The blue sedan had vanished.

"I'll keep an eye on the exits," Frank said.

They drove for another thirty minutes but still couldn't find the blue sedan. Mangieri could have taken any number of exits heading in any number of directions.

"Head back to Bayport," Frank said after another fifteen minutes.

"What?" Joe shouted.

"Mangieri would have headed back to Bayport as soon as possible."

"Give me one good reason why. We're not going to give up searching for Dad!"

"We're not giving up searching for Dad. Use

your head, Joe. Mangieri has only one place to go—Bayport!''

Joe let up on the accelerator and slowly eased the emergency brake down. The van slowed. He steered the van toward an exit. Frank made sense. Mangieri would have to head back to Bayport because that was where Stewart had to be—if Stewart was going to make good on his threat of killing all the Hardys and their friends.

''Where to now?'' Joe asked as they entered Bayport.

The sky had darkened as heavy, black rain clouds closed out the sun. A light drizzle was falling. Joe flipped on the headlights.

Frank had ridden in silence, forcing himself to shut out the image of his father in the hands of Stewart.

What would drive a man to such extremes to achieve murder? Revenge? Bobby must have kept in touch with his father over the years he was in prison. Mock's hatred for Fenton Hardy festered into a madness that had infected his son, Bobby. A blood law, Joe had called it.

''What did Leonard Mock say just before he collapsed?'' Frank asked, staring ahead through the water-spotted windshield.

Joe flipped on the windshield wipers. ''What are you talking about?''

''He said something about everything coming full circle. What do you think he meant?''

Joe glanced at Frank. "He was talking about his son."

"Maybe not just his son. The shoot-out with Leonard Mock took place at the old National Guard Armory," Frank stated matter-of-factly.

"You think that's where Stewart, I mean Bobby, has taken Dad."

"That's exactly what I think!"

Bayport's old National Guard Armory was on the city's southeast edge. The Hardys were determined that it wouldn't become their father's place of execution.

They reached the large brick and stone building in under three minutes. From the outside, the armory looked like a medieval fortress, complete with towers and ramparts. Frank and Joe had often joked about the old-fashioned design of the building, but their jokes didn't seem funny right then.

Joe shut off the headlights a half mile from the armory. He turned off the engine and let the van coast in, parking it a hundred yards from the front of the building.

"If I remember right," Frank said, "the fight with the police took place behind the armory at the old practice range."

Frank and Joe trotted around to the side, then pressed themselves against the building as they neared the practice range.

Thunder rumbled. The drizzle turned into a

trickle. The sky darkened more, and it looked like dusk rather than late morning.

The ground was still muddy from the rain the tornado had dumped, and now it was becoming even more sodden and difficult to walk through.

"There's the sedan," Frank said as they turned a corner of the building.

The blue car sat with its trunk lid open. Frank checked the inside. He found a small smear of blood and a tie clip he recognized as his father's.

"They've got him," Frank said grimly.

They reached the end of the side of the armory. Frank moved his head slowly around the corner.

"Take a look," Frank said to Joe, and they exchanged places.

Joe peeked around the corner.

A little flame flared. Mangieri's face was cast in an orange and yellow glow. He was leaning against the wall ten yards down from them. He brought the lighter up to a cigarette that dangled from his mouth and lit it. He turned away and stared to his left.

"He's mine," Joe whispered to Frank.

"Be my guest," Frank replied.

Joe slid around the corner and crept up on the unsuspecting thug. Mangieri's attention was directed in the opposite direction.

Joe tapped Mangieri on the shoulder.

"Got the time?" Joe asked with venom.

Mangieri turned and gasped. A split second later

he fired a broad right fist into the center of Joe's stomach. Joe countered with a right of his own. Mangieri fell back against the wall and slid down into the mud, the lit cigarette still dangling from his lower lip.

Joe rubbed his knuckles. "He's not going anywhere for a while," he said with a smile as Frank joined him.

Frank patted Mangieri's leather jacket to check for a gun. "Empty," he told Joe.

"Too bad," Joe said.

They continued along the back of the building until they reached the far corner.

"The practice range," Frank announced. He peered around the corner, then gasped. "Dad!" Frank whispered, trying to suppress a shout.

Fenton Hardy was tied to a lamppost some fifty yards away, his hands tied over his head, the rope hanging from a hook. His head hung down, his feet slightly off the ground. The glare from the light and the drizzle of rain created an eerie halo about him, giving him a ghostlike appearance.

"I don't see Stewart," Frank told Joe.

They moved out slowly, hoping the darkness of the oncoming storm would hide them long enough to make a run for their father.

They were halfway to him when Stewart suddenly appeared, the deadly .357 magnum hanging at his side.

Frank and Joe froze.

"I've been waiting for you."

The boys moved slowly toward him, keeping their eyes on him and the magnum at his side. They stopped at the edge of the circle of light.

Fenton raised his head. "I'm okay," he said weakly to Frank and Joe.

"Shut up!" Stewart barked.

Fenton slumped forward again.

Frank and Joe moved a step closer to Stewart.

The magnum was up and fired instantly, mud splattering Frank and Joe.

"That was just a warning. The next shot drops one of you dead."

"Let—them—go," Fenton groaned.

"Say, 'please.' " Frank and Joe were stunned to hear Stewart's childlike voice.

Stewart laughed again. This time it was more hysterical and higher-pitched. Stewart reached into his raincoat pocket and pulled out the black ski mask, which he slipped over his head.

"You don't need the disguise anymore, Bobby," Frank said.

"I'm disappointed in you, Frank. You have such a brilliant, logical mind. This isn't a disguise. It's an executioner's hood."

"You're not going to get away with this," Joe said with great control.

Stewart's laugh was just as hysterical, just as high-pitched as before.

"An empty threat from an empty head. You

should have spent more time exercising the muscle between your ears, Joe Hardy.''

Frank reached out and grabbed Joe before the younger Hardy could make a move toward Stewart.

"You see," Stewart said gleefully, "Frank is the smart one."

"If you're wearing an executioner's hood, what are the charges, when was the trial and the sentencing?" Frank glanced quickly at Joe and moved his eyes toward Stewart.

Play the game, Frank was telling Joe. Play the game.

"You want charges?" Stewart shouted. "I'll gave you charges." Stewart held up a finger. "One: sticking his nose into other people's business." He held up a second finger. "Two: causing a father and son to be separated for life." A third finger went up. "Three: putting that father in prison until he rots and dies from cancer."

Stewart began to pace in front of Fenton Hardy, all the time uncurling and curling his fingers around the pistol grip of the .357 magnum.

"This is the trial!" Stewart bellowed, his voice more agitated. "I, the jury, find Fenton Hardy guilty on all charges, the most serious of which is causing a son to be torn from his father."

Stewart paced for a few seconds more, then suddenly stopped, his back to Fenton. He turned slowly, raised the magnum shoulder level, and aimed it at Fenton's head.

He spoke softly, almost in rhythm to the drizzle that fell about them.

"The sentence: death. Just as my father was sentenced to death. The sentence to be carried out immediately."

Stewart squeezed the trigger.

"No!" Joe shouted and lunged at Stewart, the gun exploding as Joe and Stewart fell into the mud.

Joe gagged and spit out a small amount of mud. He grabbed Stewart's gun hand and pressed it deeper into the mud. The magnum erupted again, and Joe felt the recoil and the heat of the explosion. Joe pushed himself up with his left hand and hit Stewart with a right cross. Stewart groaned once and relaxed.

Joe was trying to pull the gun from Stewart's grip when the man suddenly kicked up and caught Joe in the side with his knee. Joe groaned and almost fell over. He caught himself instead and planted another solid right to Stewart's cheek.

A gasp came from Stewart, and this time he lay still, the .357 sliding from his hand and into the mud. Joe scooped up the gun and stepped back from the unconscious man. He glanced over at Frank.

Frank was untying his father. He tugged at the last knot, and the rope slackened. Fenton began to fall, but Frank caught him and helped him to stand.

"You okay, Dad?" Joe asked.

"Yes," Fenton Hardy answered weakly but with a smile.

Joe took the rope that had bound his father and tied Stewart's hands together.

"Dad needs to get to the hospital," Frank said. "I'll bring the van around."

"I can make it," Mr. Hardy said. When Frank let go, though, Fenton fell back. Frank reached out to steady his father.

"I'll help him," Joe said. "Go get the van."

"I'll call the police," Frank said as he started for the van.

Lightning flashed across the sky, followed close by thunder, and then the rain began to fall in large, hard drops.

Fenton Hardy had only minor cuts and bruises and was treated and released from the hospital.

Three days later he was sitting in his favorite easy chair drinking a cup of coffee. Frank sat on the couch with Callie and Joe. Liz and Don were on the floor, and they were all watching the news on WBAY.

"And the judge refused to set bail for Robert Edward Stewart until the former Bayport police officer could undergo a psychiatric examination by a court-appointed physician."

Frank hit the Mute button on the remote control.

"Why?" Callie asked as she took the remote control away from Frank.

"Stewart's lawyer has made a motion to plead Stewart insane," Frank explained.

Chet entered from the kitchen, a large sub in his hands.

"Who's insane?" Chet asked as he chomped down on the sandwich.

"We are, for letting you eat us out of house and home," Joe replied when he saw the four-inch thick sandwich.

"I'm still amazed at the timing and the planning involved," Callie said.

Mr. Hardy stirred. "Leonard Mock was one of the most methodical crooks I've ever dealt with."

"Mangieri supplied Mock with the photos and news clippings," Frank added. "Mangieri turned state's evidence and signed a confession, but this time he didn't get any deal."

"Mock learned who had adopted his son and sent him letters over the years," Fenton said. "He blamed me for separating them." Mr. Hardy set his cup down and stood. "I'm going to pick up Con from the hospital and drive him home. You kids try to stay out of trouble while I'm gone," he said, raising one eyebrow before walking out of the room.

"The editor really liked my story," Liz said. "Thanks, Frank."

"No problem," Frank replied.

"What about me?" Joe asked, pretending to be hurt.

"You, too, Joe," Liz said with a laugh.

"Hey, look!" Chet mumbled, with a mouthful of sub, pointing with the half-eaten sandwich at the big-screen TV.

Joe Hardy appeared on the fifty-two-inch screen in living color, his blond hair plastered to his head like a wet mop, his clothes soaked and hanging on his body like rags.

Suddenly the sound blared from the stereo speakers.

"And now, news from the fashion world," the commentator was saying. "Joe Hardy, Bayport's most eligible teenage bachelor, was caught modeling the latest in tornado attire recently in downtown Bayport."

"Hey!" Joe shouted and turned his blue eyes on Callie.

Callie, the remote control in one hand, jumped up and hit the Eject button on the videotape player. She grabbed the tape that slid out and held it up.

"Looks like Newshawk Shaw captured another exclusive!" she said with a laugh.

"Give me that tape, Callie Shaw!" Joe demanded, jumping up and chasing her from the living room while the others rolled with laughter.

Frank and Joe's next case:

Surf's up in Hawaii, and the Hardy boys are riding a crime wave into danger! Somebody's trying to deep-six champion surfer Jade Roberts, and Frank and Joe are determined to keep her from going under.

From Waikiki to Diamond Head, the Hardys find themselves in hot pursuit of a powerful crime boss. In the face of bullet-spraying motorboats and killer copters, they run the risk of suffering the worst wipeout of their lives . . . in *Fright Wave*, Case #40 in The Hardy Boys Casefiles™.